FIRESTORM!

"I have sixty-five," the auctioneer was saying. "Who'll bid seventy? Sixty-five thousand dollars, going once—going twice—and sold, for sixty-five thousand dollars!"

The people in the crowd started to clap, but suddenly their applause was silenced by a shrill scream.

Frank spun around. A thin trail of smoke was trickling out of the barn. One of the side windows was lit by a flickering glow. As Frank started to run across the riding ring, he saw a tiny figure in the opening to the hayloft. It was Samantha, Colonel Burroughs's eight-year-old daughter.

"Help, fire!" she cried. "Fire! Save me! *Save me!*"

Books in THE HARDY BOYS CASEFILES™ Series

THE HARDY BOYS

NO.
96

CASEFILES

AGAINST ALL ODDS

FRANKLIN W. DIXON

EAU CLAIRE DISTRICT LIBRARY

AN ARCHWAY PAPERBACK
Published by POCKET BOOKS
New York   London   Toronto   Sydney   Tokyo   Singapore

103706

AN ARCHWAY PAPERBACK *Original*

 An Archway Paperback published by
POCKET BOOKS, a division of Simon & Schuster Inc.
1230 Avenue of the Americas, New York, NY 10020

Copyright © 1995 by Simon & Schuster Inc.
Produced by Mega-Books, Inc.

All rights reserved, including the right to reproduce
this book or portions thereof in any form whatsoever.
For information address Pocket Books, 1230 Avenue
of the Americas, New York, NY 10020

ISBN: 0-671-88207-4

First Archway Paperback printing February 1995

10 9 8 7 6 5 4 3 2 1

THE HARDY BOYS, AN ARCHWAY PAPERBACK
and colophon are registered trademarks of Simon & Schuster Inc.

THE HARDY BOYS CASEFILES is a trademark of
Simon & Schuster Inc.

Cover art by Brian Kotzky

Printed in the U.S.A.

IL 6+

AGAINST ALL ODDS

Chapter

1

JOE HARDY PAUSED just inside the gate of the Bayport Fairground. "Wow!" he exclaimed. "Look at the crowd. I didn't know there were so many fans of steeplechase racing around here. Do you think we'll get to our seats before the race starts?"

"Sure," his older brother, Frank, replied, his dark eyes studying the crowd. At six-one he could easily see over most of the spectators' heads.

"I'm so excited," Vanessa Bender said, squeezing Joe's arm. "To think that we're going to get to watch my absolute favorite horse! I just hope he wins. That'll make the day perfect."

Joe grinned. He and Vanessa had been dating

1

since she moved to Bayport, and he'd never seen her look forward to anything as much as this race.

"The paper today said that Against All Odds is expected to finish well, so maybe you'll get your wish," Callie Shaw, Frank's long-time girlfriend, reminded Vanessa.

Vanessa pushed her long, ash-blond hair out of her eyes. "Even if he doesn't, just seeing him run will be terrific. Wasn't it nice of Colonel Burroughs to invite us to watch from the owners' enclosure? It's not as if he knows us. All I did was write him a fan letter."

The announcer's voice boomed through the loudspeaker. "Ladies and gentlemen, welcome to Bayport's very own steeplechase event. It's a grand day for racing. Today's course is two miles and four furlongs over twelve fences."

"Let's hurry," Joe said. "We don't want to miss the beginning."

Vanessa glanced at her watch and shook her head. "It's just twelve-thirty. We've got at least half an hour. Where do you think the owners' enclosure is?"

Joe shrugged. "The last time I was here was for the Harvest Carnival, and it was full of clowns and jugglers. This doesn't look like a cotton-candy crowd," he added, glancing at the well dressed spectators, many of them in boots, riding pants, and tweed riding jackets.

"It's probably over there, next to the judges' tower," Frank said, pointing. "Let's give it a shot."

Joe and the two girls followed Frank through the friendly crowd. Their goal was a grassy area surrounded by a white rail fence right next to the track. Inside, they could see several dozen people talking in small groups or sitting around wooden tables. In the far corner a big market umbrella shaded a table laden with platters of food.

"Pretty ritzy," Joe murmured to Vanessa as the teens made their way around the enclosure to the gate.

She gave him an absent-minded smile, and he realized that she was thinking only of the race and her horse's chances.

As they started through the gate, a middle-aged man in riding clothes hurried over. He wasn't very tall, but he was as solid as a concrete block. His hair was cut in a military-style crewcut, and his skin was creased like old leather. "Hold it," he said, barring the way. "Can I help you?"

Vanessa smiled. "We're here as guests of Colonel Burroughs. My name's Vanessa Bender, and these are friends of mine."

"Nice try, young lady," the man replied. "But I'll have to ask you to leave. I'm Colonel Burroughs, and I've never heard of you in my life."

Vanessa stared at him, then fumbled through her purse and produced a folded piece of stationery. "There must be some mistake," she said, her eyes flashing. "Here's the letter you sent me."

The man didn't even look at it. "I repeat, I don't know you or your friends, and I certainly didn't invite you to the owners' enclosure. Please leave without any further disturbance."

Joe stepped forward and took the letter from Vanessa. Unfolding it, he said, "This letter is from Colonel Brian Burroughs, U.S. Army, retired, of Brian Boru Farm. Is that you, sir?"

The man's face reddened. "Yes, it is," he conceded. "But I'm telling you for the last time—"

Frank asked, "Could the invitation have slipped your mind, sir? Or could somebody else have written it and forgotten to tell you?"

Burroughs glared at Frank for a moment. Then without warning he executed a flawless about-face and barked, "Helen! I need you here, please."

Joe saw a woman in a colorful flowered silk dress focus on Burroughs, then start toward him. A small girl in a white sailor dress and a straw hat trailed after her.

Burroughs stepped aside and motioned for Vanessa and her friends to come inside the fence. "No need for us to block the entrance," he said gruffly. "We'll soon sort this out."

The woman in the flowered dress came up to him and said, "Yes, darling? What is it?"

4

"This young lady is, um—" He gazed expectantly at Vanessa, who gave her name again.

"She seems to think I invited her and her friends to join us today," the colonel continued. "Do you know anything about this?"

"Of course I do," the woman said, offering her hand to Vanessa. "Hello, my dear. I'm Helen Papadoulos, Brian's fiancée, and this is Brian's daughter, Samantha. I'm so glad you could come. Brian and I were so pleased to get that kind note you sent. Weren't we, darling?" She flashed a smile at Colonel Burroughs.

"So you do know about this?" Colonel Burroughs rumbled.

"Of course, darling," she replied. "I just said so."

"And you invited her and her friends to the owners' enclosure today?" he continued.

"Naturally," Helen replied.

"Why, may I ask?" he demanded.

Helen put her hand on Vanessa's shoulder. "She's a fan, Brian. She's been following Against All Odds's career for years. She even wrote a term paper about him."

"I see," Burroughs said huffily. "Well, in that case—"

Vanessa stepped in and introduced Callie, Joe, and Frank.

Burroughs raised his eyebrows. "Hardy?" he

5

said. "You're not related to Fenton Hardy, the private investigator, are you?"

"He's our dad," Joe said proudly.

"A good man," Burroughs said, nodding decisively. "He exposed a gun-smuggling ring in my unit a few years ago, when I was still in the military. Well, if you'll excuse me, I'd better go check on my horse." He turned and marched off.

Callie focused on Helen and said, "*Papadoulos* is an unusual name. You wouldn't happen to be the painter, would you?"

Helen beamed. "How very flattering! Have you seen my work?"

"Sure," Callie said. "A couple of your horse paintings were in a gallery show last year, and the Bayport Museum has one of your dog paintings on exhibit. Are you still doing them?"

Helen smiled. "No, I've moved on," she said. "Now I'm doing a series on African wild animals. But we can talk about that later, after the race. Right now, I'm afraid there are one or two people I have to speak to. Please make yourselves at home," she added, gesturing toward the table of hors d'oeuvres.

Joe nodded toward the table and announced, "I'm starved. What do you say?"

"Let's do it," Frank replied with a grin.

The four teens edged through the crowd and picked up paper plates, then made their way along the length of the table. Joe selected finger sandwiches of ham, turkey, and roast beef, then dabbed them with horseradish sauce.

"Try the little puff pastries," Vanessa urged him, pointing to one of the platters. "They've got blue cheese inside. Delicious!"

Callie speared a shrimp with a toothpick and dipped it into cocktail sauce, then looked around. "Where are the betting windows?" she asked.

"There's no betting on steeplechase races in this country," Vanessa told her. "That's why some people call it the good twin to flat track racing."

Frank looked up from the cheese tray and asked, "Where did the name steeplechasing come from, anyway?"

"It goes back a couple of hundred years," Vanessa replied. "In Ireland and England, people used to race horses from one village to another. The horses would have to jump over hedges and fences and even streams. And the riders knew where to go by looking for the steeple of the village church. Oh, look," she added, new excitement in her voice. "The horses are coming! Quick, let's get next to the fence so we can see."

They joined the flow of the crowd toward the track and found space at the railing.

"That gray one in front is Against All Odds," Vanessa told them.

Joe craned his neck. A stable hand was leading the gray stallion, one hand clasped on the bridle.

The magnificent animal walked with its head up, proudly displaying the white blaze on its face, its ears pricked up at attention. Shoulder muscles rippled smoothly under the animal's tight skin. Against All Odds was clearly a champion.

Colonel Burroughs was striding along beside his horse. A small man with curly dark hair and a sharp, pointed nose was walking next to him. He wore white riding pants, a silk shirt of green and blue, and shiny black boots. He carried a helmet and riding crop in his hand.

"Is the guy next to Burroughs the jockey?" Callie asked.

Vanessa nodded. "His name is Nick Alexander, but everyone calls him Fast Nick. He's been riding Against All Odds for years."

Frank said, "That black horse right behind him is huge."

"That's Jackie Straight," Vanessa told him. "He's favored to win."

"He looks tough," Joe said.

"He is, but Against All Odds has a secret weapon," Vanessa confided.

Joe looked over at her. "Really? What?"

"It's not really a secret," Vanessa said. "But Against All Odds has tunnel vision. He can see only what's straight in front of him, not what's to one side or the other. That's an advantage, because he doesn't get distracted by the other horses or by the crowd."

"Like wearing blinders," Frank said.

Vanessa nodded. "Right. But steeplechase horses aren't allowed to wear blinders. Some owners tried to get Against All Odds disqualified because of his tunnel vision, but the judges ruled in his favor."

"With an advantage like that, he ought to win for sure," Joe said.

"I hope so," Vanessa said. "But he's a little smaller than the others, which doesn't help when you're jumping fences, and he's getting old. This is his seventh season. Some people have said that it's risky for him to be racing still. If he shattered a leg, they'd have to put him down—kill him—right on the track. It would be ghastly."

After all the horses had paraded past the crowd, the jockeys mounted and lined up at the start. Some of the animals pawed the ground restlessly. Others stood as still as carvings.

The announcer's voice boomed out. "Ladies and gentlemen, the flag is up. They're moving into line. We've got a dry track and perfect conditions, and we should see a very fast race. Ready—and—*they're off!*"

To Joe it was as if the horses moved from zero to sixty miles per hour. They didn't move as ten separate animals, but as one. At first short and thick, the pack grew longer and narrower as it neared the bend. The hooves beat the ground sounding like a drum corps. The jockeys, crouching forward, slapped their crops rhythmically against the horses' flanks.

Joe could barely hear the announcer's voice over the roar of the crowd. "Jackie Straight is off to an early lead. Like the Wind is second, followed by Garden Variety Cabbage. Against All Odds is fourth as they go over the first hurdle." The majestic animals barely broke stride as they leapt over the fence.

"They're moving along well as they make their way into the first turn. Like the Wind is pinching for first, but Jackie Straight is battling to keep his lead. This is a close race. And Against All Odds is moving up through the pack on the outside."

Vanessa climbed onto the rail of the fence and began yelling, "Go, Against All Odds. Go!" But Joe noted that her voice was only one of thousands screaming for a favorite. Everyone in the owners' enclosure was going crazy. Little Samantha, who was sitting on Helen's shoulders, clapped her hands and shrieked.

"Over the fourth fence and Jackie Straight still leads, with Garden Variety Cabbage threatening for second," the announcer continued, excitement building in his voice. "Against All Odds and Like the Wind are neck and neck, battling for third, followed by Sunbeam, Lucky Lucy, and Hope It Kills Me. They take the fifth jump and they're headed into the back stretch."

As the pack of horses disappeared behind a stand of fir trees, Joe took his eyes away from the track and glanced at Vanessa. Her blue-gray eyes were shining, and her cheeks were bright red.

The announcer continued to tell the crowd what was happening on the far side of the course. "Garden Variety Cabbage is feeling the strain and starting to fall back. Around the top of the turn and—*what's this?* Against All Odds is pushing hard. Passing Cabbage, Passing Wind. Pulling up on Jackie Straight."

Vanessa grabbed Joe's shoulder and climbed up to the second rail of the fence. "Go, Against All Odds!" she shouted. *"Go!"*

The pack was in sight again. Joe could just make out the blue and green of Fast Nick's racing silks. Against All Odds was first and seemed to be increasing his lead. Joe banged his fist on the fence and yelled.

"Against All Odds is breaking away," the announcer shouted. "He's got a length—a length and a half. What an amazing race!"

Fast Nick was crouched forward, all his weight on the stirrups, bringing the crop down on Against All Odds's flank in rhythm with the horse's steps.

They shot over the next hedge like a missile, but even before they hit the ground, Joe sensed that something was wrong. As Against All Odds landed, his forelegs started to buckle. Fast Nick, riding aggressively high in the saddle, flew forward and to the right. Vanessa let out a scream and started to tumble backward off the railing.

Joe steadied her, but Vanessa's earlier words were running through his mind. A racehorse that broke a leg on the track would be killed on the spot. It looked as if Against All Odds was going down.

Chapter

2

FRANK CLUTCHED the top rail of the fence, trying to follow the events on the track. As Against All Odds's forelegs buckled, Fast Nick grabbed the mane and jerked the animal's head up, shifting his own center of gravity to the rear. Momentum drove the stallion forward, and by the second step he'd regained his stride, but Jackie Straight and Garden Variety Cabbage had already shot past him, and the finish line was less than half a mile away.

Relieved, Frank let out a deep breath. Next to him, Callie had joined Vanessa in yelling, "Go, Against All Odds!"

The announcer was shouting, too, now. "As they come into the final stretch, it's Jackie

13

Straight, followed by Garden Variety Cabbage. Against All Odds is third, but charging strong on the inside rail. Over the eleventh fence, and Against All Odds moves into second. He's gaining ground in a relentless drive, challenging Jackie Straight. These horses are matching one another stride for stride. What a race this is!"

From his place at the fence, Frank could hear the thunderous hooves near the finish line. Jackie Straight and Against All Odds had pulled away from the rest of the group. Both their jockeys were riding high, flailing away with their crops.

"Over the last hurdle," the announcer panted. "They're moving hard. Against All Odds is ahead by a nose—no, Jackie's moving up. They are so close—and they cross the finish line neck and neck, followed by Garden Variety Cabbage in third!"

Vanessa didn't wait for the announcer to finish. She ran for the gate, with Frank, Joe, and Callie close behind. They caught up with her as she reached the paddock. Nick had already dismounted, covered with mud and breathing heavily. He pushed his goggles up, leaving a startling white mask around his eyes, and bent over to rub his calves.

Colonel Burroughs was on his knees next to Against All Odds, inspecting the horse's front legs. His hands were bright with blood.

"Is he all right?" Vanessa demanded, in a quavering voice.

"I think so," Burroughs answered, without raising his head. "His shins are a little greasy—bloody, that is—but I've seen worse."

"He acts nervous," Vanessa continued. "Isn't he favoring his left front leg?"

Burroughs shook his head and got to his feet. "That's just excitement. His knees are fine. That's what I was worried about, the way Nick was pushing him up on the inside rail. Nick, never push an old horse that hard."

The compact jockey glanced at his boss. "He made it, didn't he?" he objected.

Before Burroughs could reply, there was a burst of static from the loudspeakers, followed by the announcer's voice. "Ladies and gentlemen, the official winner of the steeplechase and the fifty-thousand-dollar purse is—Against All Odds!"

"Yay!" screamed Callie and Vanessa at the same time. As the crowd cheered, Vanessa gave Joe a big hug. Frank watched Fast Nick throw his arms up in the air like a victorious Olympian.

Colonel Burroughs smiled and patted his horse's neck. Then he said. "We'd better go to the winner's circle."

Burroughs passed the reins to a stable hand and headed across the track, followed by Fast Nick.

"What are we waiting for?" Vanessa demanded, and started after them. Frank caught Joe's eye and shrugged, then they and Callie followed Vanessa. Helen and Samantha were already in the winner's circle, along with a crowd of reporters and photographers.

"Congratulations, darling," Frank heard Helen coo as she gave the colonel a big kiss. Burroughs cleared his throat loudly, then bent down to pick up his daughter.

"Daddy, Daddy, I knew he'd win," Samantha proclaimed. "Against All Odds is the best horse in the whole world."

Joe nudged Vanessa and murmured, "She's as big a fan as you are."

"Close," Vanessa replied, smiling.

Burroughs, Helen, Samantha, and Nick walked to the center of the winner's circle, where an official was waiting with a giant horseshoe of flowers. The man said, "Colonel Burroughs, I'm pleased to bestow this winner's wreath and a check for fifty thousand dollars. Congratulations on a fine race."

Burroughs shook the official's hand as the cameras clicked away. Then he cleared his throat and said loudly, "Thank you. A true champion like Against All Odds deserved to end his career with a win."

"What?" Helen gasped.

Burroughs placed the horseshoe wreath on his

horse's neck and said, "Against All Odds has just retired from racing."

"But, Daddy!" Samantha exclaimed as the reporters crowded closer and the cameras started clicking again.

"Retired?" Nick said, bewildered. "What do you mean, retired?"

Colonel Burroughs turned to face the jockey. "I should have pulled Against All Odds out of racing last year. He's too old for steeplechasing. It was foolish of me to start him this season, but he's a champion horse. I wanted him to end his career on a high note."

A reporter stepped forward and asked, "What now, Colonel? Are you going to syndicate him?"

"I hope to," Burroughs replied.

As a babble of other questions arose, Frank turned to Vanessa. "What does that mean, syndicate him?"

"Champion racehorses can be worth a fortune as sires for colts," Vanessa told him. "People hope that they'll pass on their winning abilities to their descendants. So a syndicate, or agency, will buy the right to Odds's services as a father and then make its money back by selling the colts."

Frank nodded and glanced at the colonel just as Fast Nick stepped up and thrust his muddy face within inches of the older man's. "What about me?" Nick demanded in a voice thick with fury.

"What about you?" the colonel replied, sounding torn between anger and puzzlement.

"I've been riding that horse for five years," Nick proclaimed. "Don't I have a say in whether he retires?"

Burroughs acted astonished. "No, of course not," he said curtly.

For a moment, Frank was sure that the jockey was going to punch Burroughs. But then he got control of himself and said, "Don't do this just because he stumbled at the tenth fence, Colonel. Maybe that was my fault. He's in fine shape. I know he can finish the season with three or four more wins."

Burroughs shook his head. "Sorry, Nick, but Odds is too valuable to take any more risks. Come on, everyone—Helen, Samantha—smile for the cameras. We just watched the race of a lifetime."

The crowd was already starting to disperse. As Callie, Vanessa, and the Hardys walked to the parking lot, Vanessa said, "I'm glad we came today. If I'd missed seeing Against All Odds run his last race, and win it, too, I couldn't have forgiven myself."

The next week was a busy one for Frank and Joe. Joe spent most of his time working on a history project, and Frank was plowing through a course in statistics. They were outside on their way to the parking lot after school on Friday when Vanessa ran up to them.

"Guess what?" she said. "Against All Odds's syndication rights are being auctioned off in about an hour. Do you and Callie want to go watch?"

"Callie has volleyball practice," Frank said, "but we'll go. After watching that race last weekend, I feel like we own a part of that horse ourselves!"

Brian Boru Farm was west of town, almost in the next township. Joe parked the Hardys' new van in a field at the end of a line of cars. Then the three walked toward the riding ring that separated Burroughs's stately white house from a big red barn. A podium had been set up at one end of the ring. A small crowd waited a short distance from the podium. Some wore riding clothes, but most were dressed like prosperous business executives.

Frank spotted Burroughs near the podium, talking to a tall, bald man with the build of a boxer. Burroughs scowled at them as they approached.

"Hello, Colonel," Frank said, offering his hand. "Do you remember me? I'm Frank Hardy."

The scowl on Burroughs's face deepened. "I know," he growled. "Why are you here?"

"We wanted to watch the auction," Vanessa said. "Do you mind? We won't get in the way."

The bald man said, "The public was invited, young lady. I hope the event will live up to your expectations. My guess is that you'll see some real money change hands."

"Mr. Philpin is the president of Royal Bids Incorporated," Burroughs said dryly. "He makes his living as an optimist."

"It's a pleasure to meet you," Vanessa said, introducing herself to the auctioneer.

"This whole show was actually Philpin's idea," Burroughs continued. "I thought it would be more trouble than it was worth, but so far the only hard part was getting an appointment with the vet. This is a busy time for them."

"The vet?" Vanessa repeated, concerned. "Against All Odds isn't sick, is he?"

"Not at all," Burroughs said quickly. "We needed to verify that the horse is viable—that he can father offspring. No one's going to pay top dollar for syndication rights unless he's sure everything works the way it should. Odds went to the vet this morning, and he's in perfect health. Except for the tunnel vision, of course."

"Will that make him worth less?" Frank asked.

"On the contrary," Philpin answered. "There's a chance that his offspring will have tunnel vision also, and for steeplechasers, that's a plus. That's one of the reasons I expect the rights to bring a handsome sum."

Vanessa scanned the crowd. "Is Fast Nick around?"

Burroughs scowled. "No. That man's a fool. He's still angry with me for retiring Against All Odds. Samantha is sulking about it, too. Not to mention Helen."

"Why are they upset?" Frank asked. "I can understand about Nick. But all you're selling is syndication rights to Against All Odds. Samantha and Helen can still ride him and groom him, can't they?"

"Well, no, I'm afraid not," Burroughs confessed. He gestured toward the crowd gathered around the podium. "These people are stud ranchers. They have special equipment and staff veterinarians to keep their horses fit. Whoever buys the rights to Odds will keep him. The stay will depend on how long the horse proves useful to them. We may never see him after—"

"We're a bit behind schedule, Colonel," Philpin interrupted. "Why don't we begin?"

As the auctioneer climbed onto the podium, Frank noticed a white sedan speed up the drive and stop near the ring. Helen Papadoulos, in a broad-brimmed hat and dark glasses, climbed out and started toward the crowd.

Philpin spoke into the microphone. "We're

here to auction off syndication rights for a champion stallion, Against All Odds, the winner of a fifty-thousand-dollar purse at last week's steeplechase. Who'll start the bidding at twenty-five thousand dollars?"

A young man in a Western hat nodded.

"I have twenty-five," Philpin continued. "Who'll say thirty? And thirty-five? The bid is thirty-five thousand dollars. I'm looking for forty. Do I see forty?"

Suddenly Frank noticed Helen Papadoulos pushing her way to the front of the crowd. She climbed up onto the podium and grabbed the microphone from a startled Philpin. The audience stared in surprise.

"You people aren't bidding on just any horse," Helen blurted out into the mike. She pointed an accusing finger at the colonel. "You're bidding on something I thought the colonel cared about: an animal that's been his daughter's pet and best friend nearly all her life—practically a member of the family. I thought that man cared about Odds, and about us, too. But I was wrong. He dumped Against All Odds, and then he dumped me. I guess next he'll find a way to dump his little girl. Think about that when you place your bids. Now, if you'll excuse me, I'm going to say goodbye to Odds before one of you takes him away."

She threw the microphone down and stormed

off the podium. The shocked crowd separated to let her pass. As she headed toward the barn, Frank saw her break into a run.

Philpin picked up the mike, then looked at Burroughs. Tight lipped, the colonel nodded.

"Sorry for the interruption," Philpin said. "We're at thirty-five thousand. Do I hear forty?"

Near Frank, a woman in a dark red coat gave a tiny nod.

"And forty we have, looking for forty-five," Philpin chanted. "You're under the money on this one, ladies and gentlemen. A champion stallion in the prime of life. Who'll say forty-five?"

Frank glanced over toward the barn. He was surprised that Helen was so attached to Against All Odds. Was this auction the only reason she was so angry at Burroughs? It sounded as if something else had happened between the two of them.

When Helen emerged from the barn, she had her dark glasses in one hand. As she started toward her car, she tripped over a stone and almost fell.

Frank nudged Vanessa. "Look," he said. "I think she's crying."

"She's too upset to drive," Vanessa replied. "Maybe I ought to drive her home."

"Good idea. Where shall I meet you later?" Joe asked. "We are going out, right?"

"Sure," Vanessa replied, giving him a warm

smile. "Why don't we meet at Taco Loco, that new Mexican place at the mall? I've been wanting to try it. How's eight?"

Joe nodded and asked how she'd get home from Helen's house. "A cab or my mom," she replied, and hurried over to Helen's car. A few moments later the white sedan pulled away, with Vanessa at the wheel.

Frank turned back to the auction. "I have sixty-five," Philpin was saying. "Who'll bid seventy? Seventy? Sixty-five thousand dollars, going once—going twice—and sold, for sixty-five thousand dollars."

The people in the crowd started to clap, but suddenly their applause was silenced by a shrill scream.

Frank spun around. A thin trail of smoke was trickling out of the barn. One of the side windows was lit by a flickering glow. As Frank started to run across the riding ring with Joe at his side, he saw a tiny figure in the opening to the hayloft. It was Samantha.

"Help, fire!" she cried. "Fire! Daddy, Daddy! *Save me!*"

Chapter

3

EVEN BEFORE he and Frank darted in through the door of the burning barn, Joe could feel the force of the blaze. Inside, every gulp of air seemed to sear his throat and lungs. Joe told himself not to panic. The important thing was to rescue Samantha, and quickly, before the barn and everything in it became an inferno.

The smoke was so thick that Joe couldn't see more than a couple feet in front of him. Arms out in front of him, he groped forward, listening for Samantha's screams. He found a ladder. As he started to climb, a nearby bale of hay flashed into flame. Joe scrambled up the ladder, hoping he wouldn't meet the same fate.

The large open doors of the hayloft acted like

a chimney, drawing the smoke and heat upward. Samantha was huddled on the plank floor next to the doors. Was she already unconscious, or— Joe ran to her and knelt beside her. When he touched her, she turned and stared at him with fear-widened eyes.

"Don't worry, Samantha," Joe said, lifting her into his arms. "You'll be fine."

He started to carry her toward the ladder, but suddenly flames spurted through the opening in the floor. As Joe backed away, Samantha dug her fingers into his neck, screaming, "No, make it go away! I don't want to get burned."

Joe hugged the hysterical child. "You won't get burned," he said. "I promise."

The open door was their only chance. Staying low to avoid the poisonous fumes, Joe crept over to it and peered down. The hard dirt was twenty feet below, with nothing to cushion their jump. At best, Joe knew, he risked shattering his knees and hips. Could he be sure that his body would cushion Samantha's fall, or would he be risking her life as well?

The flames roared through the opening to the lower level, starting to ignite the bales of hay stacked nearby. There was no time for debate. Joe and Samantha might die if he jumped, but if he stayed put, they would certainly die, and in the next few minutes.

Adrenaline pumping, Joe set the sobbing Samantha on the floor and grabbed two bales of hay, which he dragged to the doorway. He tossed them out. Even before they hit the ground, he was pulling two more over, then two more. The next time he went back for more, the remaining bales were on fire. It was now or never.

Joe draped Samantha over his left shoulder in a fireman's carry. "Close your eyes and hold on tight," he told her. Then he staggered to the opening, quickly surveyed the bales on the ground below, and jumped.

The heat on the ground floor of the burning barn was intense. Frank, bent almost double, scurried toward the rear, guided by the unearthly screams of terrified horses. Their hooves kicking the wooden sides of their stalls boomed like thunder.

One by one, Frank found the wooden latches of the stalls and threw the doors open, then tugged the frantic animals out and pointed them in the direction of the barn door and safety. "Three," he muttered. "Is that all?"

As if in answer, he heard a powerful neighing from somewhere to his right. Frank groped toward it, but when he grabbed the latch, it was iron, not wood. With a yelp, he yanked his hand away. The latch was as hot as a burning stove.

Frank's eyes were stinging from smoke and from the sweat pouring down his face. He wiped his sleeve across his forehead and tried to think how to open the stall. He knew he didn't have much longer to decide.

As he tried to blink away the pain, his gaze fell on a leather harness hanging from a nail. *"Yes!"* he shouted. Racked with painful coughs, he grabbed the harness, quickly wrapped the thick leather around the latch handle, and pulled upward. The latch opened and the door to the stall swung wide.

Inside, Against All Odds reared up on his hind legs and pawed the air in terror. "Move it!" Frank yelled, slapping the horse on the flank. But the stallion saw the flames and backed farther into the stall, almost crushing Frank.

Just then Frank remembered a stable fire he'd seen in an old movie on television. What had the hero done? Remembering, Frank ripped off his shirt and wrapped it around the horse's head, tying it under the jaw in a makeshift blindfold. Instantly the horse seemed calmer.

"Okay, guy, we're out of here!" Frank shouted. At that moment one of the beams supporting the overhead loft gave way. Flaming hay and wood showered down. Without hesitating, Frank grabbed the stallion's mane with both hands, swung himself onto its back, and kicked its heaving ribs. The stallion tore out of the stall, galloping straight through the flames toward the open barn door. Frank took a deep breath of cool fresh air and felt himself slide off the horse to the ground. A rim of darkness began to form around the edge of his vision. It spread fast, closing in until he could see nothing but a small point of light. Then nothing at all.

Joe had just passed Samantha to her white-faced father when he heard a cheer go up from the crowd. He spun around and saw Frank come galloping out of the burning barn on the back of Against All Odds. As the horse slowed to a stop, Joe rushed over.

"You made it!" he shouted as Frank slid to the ground. Frank didn't answer. His face was deathly pale, and his eyes were closed.

"Somebody call an ambulance!" Joe yelled over his shoulder as he flung himself down beside his unconscious brother.

"It's on the way," someone replied.

Joe made sure Frank was breathing, then checked his heartbeat. The pulse in his neck was rapid and fluttery, but Joe didn't think that his condition called for CPR. As Joe slid his rolled-up jacket under Frank's head, he heard sirens approaching. Two fire trucks pulled up, followed closely by an emergency medical truck. As the fire fighters began shooting thousands of gallons of water into the barn, two paramedics came running with a first aid kit and an oxygen supply.

"What happened?" one of them demanded.

"He was in there too long," Joe replied, nodding toward the barn.

One medic held an oxygen mask over Frank's face, while the other put salve and gauze on his burns. A minute later Frank's eyes opened. He pushed at the mask and started to cough. When the fit passed, he met Joe's eyes and said, "The kid—is she okay?"

"She's fine," Joe said. "You're the one I'm worried about."

"I'm fine." Frank tried to sit up.

"Take it easy, pal," the medic said, pressing him back down. "You've got a bad case of smoke inhalation."

Frank shook his head. "I'll feel better sitting up."

"Your choice, pal," the medic replied. He put his arm around Frank's shoulders to help support him. Joe, on Frank's other side, took his arm.

"Have you two young idiots lost whatever sense you had?"

Joe looked around. Colonel Burroughs, hands on hips, was glaring down at them.

"Don't you mean 'Are you all right?' " Joe countered.

"Of course you're all right. I've seen lesser men hit by shrapnel and walk away from it." He pointed toward the barn. "You see those fire fighters? They're trained to run into burning buildings. You're not. Leave difficult jobs to the professionals, that's what I say. You young fools could have been killed."

"So could your daughter," Joe pointed out.

"And your horses," Frank added.

Colonel Burroughs drew himself up even straighter than usual. "Heroism is no substitute for good judgment. Is that clear?"

"Yes, sir," Frank and Joe said in unison.

Colonel Burroughs frowned. Then he said, "Thank you for saving my daughter's life." With a nod that felt almost like a salute, he turned and went to examine the horses.

Frank met Joe's eyes and said, "Was he bawling us out or thanking us?"

"Both, I think," Joe replied.

Just then Joe spotted a white van sporting a Bayport Eyewitness News logo pulling in behind the fire trucks. A man in a blue sports coat climbed out, followed by a portly guy with a video camera and a young woman carrying a boom mike and battery-powered tape recorder. They began shooting footage of the fire fighters and the burning barn.

Joe tapped Frank on the shoulder and indicated the two police cars that had also pulled up.

"Uh-oh," Frank groaned, struggling to his feet. Bayport Police Chief Ezra Collig and Officer Con Riley had climbed out of their cars and were heading over. The chief's expression as he recognized Frank and Joe made him look as if he had just eaten something foul.

"The Hardy brothers," he said, shaking his head. "I didn't need this. Why are you always in the middle of trouble?"

"Just lucky, I guess," Joe cracked.

"Are you fellows okay?" Riley asked, concerned.

"We're fine," Frank told him.

Collig buttonholed one of the fire fighters. "Do we know what caused the blaze?" he asked.

"Not yet," the man replied with a shrug. "An old wooden barn filled with hay—almost anything could have set it off. A spark from an old electrical outlet, a stray match—"

"What about arson?" the police chief demanded.

"That's for the fire marshal to say," the fire fighter replied. "Excuse me."

Collig took in the area with his eyes. One of the stable hands was giving Samantha a piggyback ride while her father inspected the horses. Collig noted Samantha's soot-blackened face. "Was that kid inside the barn?" he demanded.

Joe shrugged and said nothing.

Collig marched over to her, pulling out his notebook and pen. Joe and Frank followed him. "Hello, little girl," the chief said, in a voice as soothing as fingernails on a blackboard. "Tell me, were you playing with matches today?"

Samantha's eyes widened. She shook her head.

Collig jotted something down, then turned and headed back to his car.

"Samantha?" Frank said gently. "Did you see anyone else in the barn when you were up in the hayloft?"

Samantha looked at him with her wide eyes. "Just Aunt Helen," she told him. "But she didn't know I was there. I was hiding. Then she went away."

Frank and Joe both remembered watching Helen leave the barn. Could she have set it on fire as a way of getting revenge on her ex-fiancé?

"Let's check on Against All Odds," Frank murmured. "After all that, I'd like to be sure he's in good shape."

The Hardys walked across the yard to where Colonel Burroughs was inspecting the stallion. As they drew near, the colonel pulled a chrome lighter from his jacket, held it beside the horse's head, and flicked it. The horse neighed loudly and tried to back away.

Burroughs spun on his heel. His eyes were bulging and his face was red.

"What's the matter, Colonel?" Frank asked. "Is something wrong with Against All Odds?"

"Wrong? I'll say there is," the colonel shouted, pointing an accusing finger at the Hardys. "This horse is not Against All Odds. It's an impostor!"

33

Chapter

4

"AN IMPOSTOR?" Frank stared in disbelief at the colonel. "But that *has* to be Against All Odds! I found him in his stall and rode him out here. You saw me yourself!"

Burroughs said coldly, "My horse has tunnel vision, remember? He doesn't see things at the side."

Once more Burroughs held his cigarette lighter near the side of the horse's head and clicked it into flame. Once again, the horse whinnied, rolled its eyes, and backed away.

"This may look like Odds, but it isn't," Burroughs continued. "Somebody stole my horse, then set the barn on fire to cover up the crime. If this horse hadn't survived, we would never have discovered the substitution."

Frank noticed that the colonel was making it sound as if the horse had escaped from the barn on its own. Talk about gratitude!

Burroughs put his fists on his hips and turned to scan the crowd. "Chief Collig?" he called. "Could I speak to you?"

Collig came over slowly as though he wasn't in the habit of having people summon him. "What is it, Colonel?" he asked.

"Helen Papadoulos," Burroughs replied curtly. "I want you to arrest her at once for arson and horse theft."

Collig took out his notebook. "We need a good reason to arrest somebody," he pointed out. "What do you have against this lady?"

Burroughs explained about the horse substitution, then added, "Helen went into the barn just before the fire started. I'm positive she started it, for revenge and to cover her tracks."

Frank could tell that the police chief found this accusation very thin, but Collig went through the motions anyway. "Did anybody else notice her?" he asked.

"I did," Joe volunteered. "But I saw her leave, too, and she sure didn't have a horse with her."

"She could have swapped the horses earlier, then set the fire when she was in the barn today," Burroughs insisted.

As Chief Collig made more notes, Con Riley joined them. "Maybe we should wait for the fire marshal's report," he suggested. "If that says the fire was suspicious, then we can question Ms. Papadoulos. By the way, Colonel, how do you know her?"

Burroughs cleared his throat. "Er—we were engaged," he said, staring at the ground. "I broke it off earlier this week."

Frank saw Collig and Riley glance at each other. It wouldn't be the first time that one half of a fractured couple had accused the other of a crime.

"Thank you for your help, Colonel," Chief Collig said. "We'll keep you informed of our progress."

Frank said, "Our friend, Vanessa, drove Helen home from here. If you like, we'll drop by and ask her if she noticed anything."

"You will do no such thing," Burroughs said through clenched teeth. "This is a job for the proper authorities, not for a couple of teenagers."

"Just what I've been telling Frank and Joe for a long time," Chief Collig agreed.

Frank shrugged, hiding his resentment. "I only offered," he said. "Come on, Joe. We'd better get home. My burns are starting to hurt again."

On the way into town, Frank and Joe discussed the fire and its amazing aftermath. "I hate being ordered off a case," Joe griped. "And it's not just Chief Collig. Colonel Burroughs, the *victim,* wants us out, too."

"If he really is the victim," Frank said as Joe turned into the Hardys' driveway.

Joe set the parking brake, then turned to study Frank's face. *"If?"* he repeated. "What do you mean?"

Frank shook his head. "I'm not sure. But when somebody tries to get us off a case, I always wonder why. And the colonel spotted that substitution awfully quickly. It was almost as if he were expecting it."

"Why would he steal his own horse?" Joe demanded.

"No idea," Frank admitted. "Maybe we'll find that out when we check a little deeper."

"Then we're going to investigate?" Joe asked, relief sounding in his voice.

Frank laughed. "What do *you* think? Come on, let's get ready and head over to the mall. I'll call Callie and tell her to meet us there, too."

They ran inside to shower and change. As they were headed out again, their mother stopped them. "Where are you off to now?" Laura Hardy asked.

"We're meeting Vanessa and Callie at the mall," Frank replied.

"I don't suppose you'll be back for dinner," she said with a sigh.

"Nope, sorry," Joe said. "We're going to try that new Mexican restaurant. We won't be late. 'Bye."

Taco Loco was on the second level of Bayport Mall, sandwiched between a jeans store and a place that sold kitchen gear. It was a lively place with sombreros and serapes on the walls. From the sound system came the cheerful rhythms of a mariachi band.

Callie and Vanessa were sitting in a corner booth with a couple of other friends, Phil Cohen and Chet Morton. As Joe and Frank approached, Phil, a sturdy guy with sandy hair, said, "Eight," and bit into a pale green jalapeño pepper. His face turned red, and his eyes seemed to bulge out. He reached for his glass.

"No water allowed," Chet said with a grin. He tossed two peppers into his mouth. "Sixteen."

"It's a contest," Callie explained as the Hardys sat down. "Chet has to eat two peppers for every one Phil eats. Want to play?" She passed the bowl of peppers.

Frank shook his head. "I just came out of a fire. I don't need to put one inside me."

Callie tilted her head to one side. "What you mean?"

"There was a fire at Burroughs's farm," Frank replied. "The barn was gutted. Only the outer structure is standing."

Vanessa's face turned pale. "Is Against All Odds all right?"

Joe took her hand and said, "Yes and no. He wasn't hurt, but he's missing."

The waitress came over. Frank and Joe gave their orders, then took turns telling about the auction, the fire, and discovering that another horse had been substituted for the champion stallion. As they were finishing, the waitress appeared with a loaded tray. "Hot plates," she said, setting the sizzling platters on the table.

Vanessa didn't even glance at the food. "Where's Odds now?" she asked.

"Your guess is as good as mine," Joe replied. Then, noticing how upset Vanessa was, he added, "But I'm sure he's fine. Burroughs thinks Helen made the swap to get back at him for dumping her."

"I was with her all afternoon," Vanessa protested. "She couldn't have set the fire."

Frank crunched a tortilla chip. "She could have dropped a match as she was leaving the barn," he countered. "Or it could have been an accident."

"I can tell you one thing," Vanessa said. "She loves Burroughs, difficult as he is."

"I wonder why he broke up with her," Joe pondered, taking a sip of soda.

Vanessa avoided his eyes and said, "What if Burroughs swapped the horse himself, to get Helen in trouble?"

"And set his own barn on fire, nearly killing his kid?" Frank said.

"He wouldn't have known she'd be there," Vanessa pointed out. "Was the barn insured?"

"We don't know yet," Joe told her.

"Anyway, if we're looking for motives," Frank interjected, "Fast Nick has one, too."

"Who's that?" Chet asked.

"Burroughs's jockey," Frank explained.

"They had a big fight after the race, when Burroughs announced that Odds was going to be retired—putting Fast Nick out of a job."

"You think he stole the horse just because he was angry?" Phil asked.

"There could be more," Frank said. "Think about it. Against All Odds won fifty thousand dollars last weekend, and Burroughs gets it all, because he's the owner. If Nick stole Odds, he might be able to race him around the country under a different name and keep the winnings himself."

"What next?" Vanessa asked.

Joe shrugged. "We've got Chief Collig watching us. He told us not to talk to Helen."

"He didn't say anything about Nick, though," Frank pointed out. "Why don't we go have a little chat with him tomorrow morning?"

"Great idea," Joe said, using a tortilla chip to scoop up some refried beans.

There was only one Nick Alexander in the Bayport telephone directory. The address listed was the Bayport Marina. The next morning

Frank and Joe drove around the harbor to the boat basin.

"There must be a hundred boats docked here," Frank said as Joe pulled into the parking lot. "We'd better ask somebody which one is Nick's."

As they approached the gate to the marina, a white-haired man with a fishing rod and a tackle box was coming out.

"Excuse me," Frank said. "Do you know where we can find Nick Alexander's boat?"

"Sorry," the man replied. "But there's a directory on the wall of the guard's booth."

"Thanks," Joe said.

The guard's booth was vacant, but they found the directory. Alexander, F. N., was listed as being at Slip 18, C Dock. They followed the signs to C Dock and started along it. A lot of the boats tied up on either side were houseboats that ranged from floating shacks to floating palaces. There were also quite a few sailboats, a few big, gleaming cabin cruisers, and one cigarette boat that looked as if it were going seventy miles an hour at anchor.

The houseboat in Slip 18 was closer to a shack than a palace. The name painted on the stern was *Mount & Go*.

"Ahoy," Joe called, feeling a little silly as he said it. "It's Frank and Joe Hardy. Permission to come aboard?"

"Go away," said a voice from the far end of the boat.

"We want to talk to you," Joe insisted. He and Frank exchanged glances. "We're coming aboard."

They descended the gangplank. Nick was sitting on a fold-out chair, his feet propped up on the railing. The jockey looked even smaller in jeans than he had in his racing silks. He scowled and said. "Didn't I tell you to buzz off?"

"We'd like to ask you a few questions," Frank said. "About Against All Odds."

"I've got nothing to say," the jockey replied.

Frank suppressed a sigh. "Did you hear that he was stolen?"

"Yeah, I heard," Nick said. "Too bad."

"You had a big argument with the colonel after the race last weekend," Joe pressed. "Do you mind telling us where you were yesterday?"

Nick's face reddened and the vein in his temple began to throb. "What do you mean?" he blurted out, leaping to his feet. "You think I set fire to Burroughs's barn and stole Odds?"

Before Joe could react, the jockey reached down, grabbed a black spear gun from the deck, and aimed the glittering point straight at Joe's chest. In a seething voice, he said, "I could *kill* you for saying something like that about me!"

Chapter

5

JOE FACED FAST NICK squarely, not letting his eye stray to the gleaming spear aimed directly at him.

"You've got a problem, Nick," he said coolly. "That thing holds only one spear, and there are two of us."

"That's right," Frank said. "And one second after you shoot my brother, I'm going to snap your neck and feed your carcass to the fishes."

Nick swung the spear gun to point at Frank.

Joe said, "Now he's thinking of skewering you, Frank. But don't worry, I'll avenge you. For starters, I'll shove that gun down his throat."

The jockey shifted his gaze, and his aim, back to Joe. The moment he moved, Frank

43

attacked with a left round-kick to Nick's extended wrist.

The jockey grunted as the spear gun flew from his grasp. Frank didn't stop. He planted his left foot, bent the knee, and continued full circle, extending his right leg in a powerful wheel-kick. His heel struck Nick on the back of the calf, just below the knee. The jockey fell like a stone.

"All right, Nick," Frank said. "Do you want to talk about Against All Odds, or do you want to go a few more rounds?"

"What do you want to know?" the jockey said, staggering to his feet.

"A world-class racehorse is missing," Joe said. "Somebody torched Burroughs's barn and almost killed his daughter. Grand theft, arson, attempted murder—this is serious. And the minute we ask you a couple of questions, you threaten to turn me into shish kebab. Not good, Nick. Not good at all."

Nick collapsed in the deck chair and rubbed his injured wrist. "I just wanted to scare you," he said sullenly. "And, sure, I'm plenty sore at the colonel, but why would that make me steal Against All Odds?"

Frank took a step closer, forcing Nick to bend his head back to see Frank's face. "The other day you said that Odds is too young to retire. What's to stop you from racing him under a different name and keeping the prize money for yourself?"

Nick gave a derisive snort. "Listen, kid, you don't know beans about horse racing. Against All Odds is too famous to race under a different name. I'd never get away with it."

Frank glanced over at Joe. They hadn't thought of that.

"And here's another thing," the jockey continued. "Burroughs decided to retire the horse because he stumbled on the track, right? Well, that stumble wasn't an accident."

"What?" Joe exclaimed.

"Somebody spiked the horse," Nick said. "They drove a three-penny nail into his hoof, and it gradually worked its way into the quick. It's a miracle Odds finished the race."

"Who found the nail?" Frank asked.

"Not Burroughs, even if he is supposed to be a trainer," Nick said sourly. "I did. And I think Burroughs hobbled his own horse."

Joe said, "He won fifty thousand dollars in that race. Why sabotage that?"

"Burroughs wasn't expecting a win," Nick replied. "Odds and I won that race in spite of what he did. Besides, that fifty thousand dollars was chicken feed to Burroughs. He has Odds insured for a million. My guess is he planned to shatter the horse's leg so he could collect on the insurance. When that didn't work, he figured out a way to get the money *and* keep the horse—by putting a ringer in the stall and setting the barn on fire."

"What about Helen Papadoulos?" Frank asked.

"What about her?" Nick replied gruffly. "I hear she finally wised up to that rat and told him to buzz off."

"We hear that he broke up with her," Joe told him. "Maybe she stole the horse, to get revenge on him."

The jockey shook his head. "That's not her style. She's a class act. Listen, I've had enough of this. Why don't you just go away and leave me alone?"

After a glance at Joe, Frank said, "Okay, Nick. But we may be back."

As they walked up the dock toward the marina entrance, Joe asked, "Do you think he's telling the truth?"

Frank gave a wry smile. "Some of it. He wouldn't invent that part about the insurance policy. It's too easy to check. But as for the nail in the horse's hoof, I don't know. He's the only witness. Maybe he's just trying to come up with an excuse for his own poor riding."

"Let's try Burroughs again," Joe suggested as they climbed into the van. "It's nearly lunchtime. Maybe he'll be in a better mood to answer questions."

Twenty minutes later the Hardys parked the van near the colonel's riding ring. A smell of charred wood still lingered in the air. They went around to the front door of the big house and rang the bell. Colonel Burroughs appeared at the door.

"Well," he said in a polite but distant voice. "What brings you boys here?"

"We were in the neighborhood, so we thought we'd see how you and Samantha were recovering after yesterday," Frank said.

"We're fine, thanks," the colonel replied. After an awkward pause, he took a step back and asked them in.

The Hardys walked past Burroughs into an enormous living room. It didn't look as if the colonel needed that insurance money. He was obviously wealthy. Along the rear wall was a huge window looking out on a rolling meadow. A bearskin rug lay on the floor and a crystal chandelier hung from the ceiling.

Burroughs motioned them to sit down on a leather couch near the fireplace. He sat down in a chair opposite them.

"Is there any news about Odds?" Joe asked. "You must be worried about him."

"Worried? Not at all," the colonel snapped. "Chief Collig and his officers will find my horse and arrest the culprit."

Frank asked, "Has anybody figured out when the swap took place?"

Burroughs frowned. "That's hard to say. The horse that Philpin took to the vet was definitely Against All Odds. Dr. Tierartz checked him over from head to tail and gave him a clean bill of health."

"Do you mind giving us the vet's number?" Joe asked. "I'd like to ask him a few questions."

"I certainly would mind!" Burroughs roared in his parade-ground voice. He took a deep breath, then continued, "I know you boys mean well. And with a father like Fenton Hardy, I suppose it comes naturally to you to want to unravel mysteries. But for the last time, leave this to the proper officials."

"Oh, of course," Frank said soothingly. "But you can't blame us for being curious. We were both nearly burned to death yesterday, in your barn. Have they found out yet what caused the fire?"

The reminder that the Hardys had rescued both his daughter and his horses calmed Burroughs down. "Well, no, not yet," he said. "The police think that Samantha was playing with matches, but I know better."

"Has the fire marshal issued a report?" Frank probed.

"Not yet," Burroughs repeated. "I wish they'd

hurry up. Once they close the case, I can deal with my insurance company."

"Is Odds insured?" Frank asked in his most innocent voice. "Or just the barn?"

The colonel's face darkened. In an ominous voice he said, "Why do you ask?"

Joe leaned forward. "If you stood to collect a lot of money from Against All Odds's death, wouldn't that give you a possible motive to stage the switch?"

"I deeply resent your insinuations against my honor," the colonel said, barely containing his rage. "But I have nothing to hide. Odds is insured for a million dollars. Helen and I are joint beneficiaries of the policy. I don't know what I'll do if that crazy woman ends up getting half a million for stealing my horse."

Frank stared at Burroughs. Helen Papadoulos stood to benefit from the insurance policy on the racehorse? This was unexpected news. "Do you still think that she's involved with the disappearance?" he asked.

Colonel Burroughs jumped to his feet. "Does a one-legged duck swim in circles?" he demanded. "Of course she did it. Not only does she need the money, but she must think it's the perfect way to get back at me. And when the police prove it—as I'm sure they will—I'll make sure that she is prosecuted to the full extent of the law."

He ran his fingers through his hair. "The police will solve this," he added. "I don't want any more interference from you boys. Now I think you'd better leave."

Frank and Joe had no choice. They followed him to the front door and started across the lawn to the van. As they neared it, Samantha rode toward them on her tricycle, wearing a riding helmet and tapping the rear wheels with a stick. "Whoa!"

"Hi, Samantha," Joe said, as she stopped next to them. "That's a nice horse you're riding. What's its name?"

"Don't be silly," she replied. "This isn't a horse, it's a tricycle."

"That's right, Joe," Frank said with a wink. "Don't you know that horses don't have wheels?" He turned back to Samantha. "I bet you've answered a lot of questions about what happened yesterday."

"The police think I was playing with matches," she said matter-of-factly. "But I wasn't. Playing with matches is dumb."

Frank smiled. "That's right. Did anybody come into the barn while you were there?"

"Just Aunt Helen," Samantha replied. "But I hid so she wouldn't see me."

Something about her answer sounded odd to Frank. "Why did you hide from Helen?" he asked. "Aren't you two still friends?"

Samantha scuffed the dirt with the toe of her shoe. "Sure, we're friends," she said. "But I didn't want her to see me and find out I'd left the house after she told me not to."

Frank shot a glance at Joe. "Helen told you not to leave the house?" he asked. "When, Samantha?"

"The day before," the child replied. "She told me to stay in the house the whole time and not to go near the barn."

Chapter

6

"HELEN MUST BE THE ONE," Joe said, pacing back and forth in the Hardys' living room. "It's obvious, right? She was upset that Colonel Burroughs dumped her. She probably stole Against All Odds just to embarrass him. She must have figured that the vet would notice that it was the wrong horse, making the colonel out to be an idiot. But the vet didn't catch on."

Joe frowned to himself, then continued. "When she realized that the auction was going ahead, she had to come up with a new plan. She warned Samantha to stay out of the barn, then set it on fire. The idea was that the ringer would be destroyed and that she'd come out of it in the clear, with half a million in insurance money in her pocket."

"Not bad, as theories go," Frank said. "But there's not a scrap of proof for it. Besides, it doesn't make very good psychological sense. You're saying she started out planning a practical joke, found out that it had misfired, and immediately came up with a different scheme that meant committing arson, theft, insurance fraud, and who knows what? That's pretty radical."

"Have any better ideas?" Joe demanded.

Frank shrugged. "Not yet. But I can't help thinking that Burroughs is involved in this. He's taking the loss of his champion stallion too calmly. And why does he keep telling us to butt out of the investigation?"

"We're not *professionals*," Joe said with a chuckle. "How about this? Maybe he and Helen are in it together. Maybe the whole breakup was just a smokescreen."

Frank thought for a moment, then shook his head. "Too farfetched," he said.

"Maybe," Joe conceded. "But one thing's definite."

"What's that?" Frank asked.

Joe laughed grimly. "We're overdue for a talk with Helen Papadoulos."

"Good idea," Frank said with a nod. "But first I think we should talk to the vet. He might be able to help us figure out exactly when Against All Odds was swapped."

They found Dr. Tierartz's address in the phone

book and drove to his office. The waiting room was brightly lit with fluorescent overheads and smelled of disinfectant. A man with bright red hair, wearing a white lab jacket, opened an inner door and said, "Take a seat. I won't be long."

Joe and Frank sat on one of the two long wooden benches and waited. After a few minutes the inner door opened again. A man carrying a cocker spaniel came out, followed by the red-haired man.

"She'll be fine now," the man told the dog owner. "But next time tell her to open the jar of leftovers, instead of knocking it to the floor and then eating the broken glass."

The dog owner laughed. "I'll do my best," he promised. "Thanks, Bill." He left, and the veterinarian turned to Joe and Frank with a quizzical expression.

"Doctor Tierartz?" Joe asked. "I'm Joe Hardy and this is my brother, Frank."

"The detectives?" Tierartz replied. "I've followed a couple of your cases in the paper. Come on in. What can I do for you?"

The Hardys followed him into his office and sat down. "Have you heard about what happened at Colonel Burroughs's farm yesterday?"

"I certainly did," the vet replied. "What a catastrophe!"

"We're trying to find Against All Odds,"

Frank explained. "You examined the horse yesterday, before the auction, didn't you?"

"That's right," Tierartz said. "Why?"

Frank said, "We're hoping to pin down the time when the substitution was made."

"I see." The vet rubbed his chin. "So you'd like to know if the horse I examined was Against All Odds without a doubt, or if the switch might have already been made."

"Right," Frank said. "If you're certain that you examined Odds, then the swap must have been made right before or during the auction. But if you're not sure, it could have happened any time last week."

"Well, well," Tierartz said. He stood up, went to one of the file cabinets, and pulled out a folder. "Here's his chart," he said. "Everything normal, except a severely restricted ocular field."

"What's that mean?" Joe asked.

"Tunnel vision," the doctor replied. "The horse I examined was Against All Odds. No doubt about it."

"What's the latest on that missing horse?" Laura Hardy asked as the brothers were finishing dinner.

"Not much," Frank admitted. "We spoke to the vet this afternoon, and he's positive the horse he examined before the auction was Against All Odds."

"So the swap was made during the auction," Fenton Hardy deduced. "If you're right, then anyone who was there the whole time has an alibi."

"Who wasn't there?" Aunt Gertrude asked.

"Fast Nick, the jockey," Joe said. "And he has a motive."

"And since Helen Papadoulos came late," Frank pointed out, "she could have taken Odds out through the back of the barn and hidden him somewhere, then brought the other one in before driving back for her big scene."

"She'd probably need a helper," Fenton noted.

"We can ask her," Joe said. He stood up and began to stack the dishes. "I say tonight is as good a time as any."

After loading the dishwasher, Frank and Joe got in the van for the fifteen-minute drive to Helen Papadoulos's house. It turned out to be a cottage in a wooded area outside of Bayport, not too far from the farmhouse where Vanessa lived.

Frank and Joe walked up the path to the front door. "I don't see any lights," Joe said as he rang the bell.

Frank pushed the bell again. "The house has that empty sound. Let's check the garage."

They circled the house. The garage door was down, but through the window they could see that there was no car inside.

"What do you say?" Joe asked. "Come back another time?"

"Well, since we're here . . ." Frank said slowly. "Maybe we ought to look around."

They collected some tools from the van, then went around to the back door. While Joe held the flashlight, Frank fastened a ratchet-clip onto the lock, then inserted the medium probe. It took a little coaxing to get the tumblers in place. As soon as he felt the fourth one go down, Frank turned the ratchet-clip, and the dead bolt slid free. He glanced at the luminescent dial of his watch. "Ninety-three seconds."

"Not bad," Joe conceded. He followed Frank inside. Using their flashlights as little as possible, the Hardys crossed the kitchen, made a quick search of the dining room, and went into what was clearly Helen's studio.

"Wow!" Joe said, focusing his light on a big painting of a tiger. "She's good, isn't she?"

The paintings were almost more realistic than a photograph. About half of the pictures were of tigers. The others were of horses, dogs, and other animals. There was one of an elephant.

"I wonder how much the elephant charged her to pose," Frank cracked.

Joe pointed his flash at an old rolltop desk in the corner of the studio. "The answer's probably there," he said.

The lock on the desk took Frank less than ten

seconds to open. He rolled the lid up and he and Joe began to go through the papers inside. Nothing but letters, bills, and invitations to gallery openings.

Joe found her checkbook and scanned the register. "Look at this, Frank," he said. "On Thursday she wrote a check for almost a hundred dollars to Harry's Feed Store. If you kidnap a horse, you've got to feed it, right?"

"I imagine," Frank said. He pulled a tiny camera from his shirt pocket, adjusted the flash, and snapped two photos of the checkbook page.

After finishing their search of the studio, the Hardys followed a long hall to the bedroom.

"Don't close the door," Frank said. "We want to be able to hear if anyone is coming."

Joe shrugged, then crossed the room and tugged open the closet door. He found a wool jacket, a pair of paint-splattered overalls, and a few skirts, blouses, and dresses, but nothing that could be used as a clue.

"Joe, look at this!" Frank exclaimed.

"What?" Joe joined Frank at the dresser and peeked over his shoulder. Frank held up a photograph in an elegant frame. It was of Helen, standing very close to Fast Nick on the deck of his boat. They looked very happy.

"Would she keep this on her dresser if she and Nick were just friends?" Frank wondered aloud.

"I don't know," Joe replied. "But I don't see

any pictures of the colonel. I think we may be onto something here."

"Hold this while I take a picture," Frank said, handing the photo to Joe and taking out the camera again.

Frank took two pictures. Then he began flipping through the dresser drawers while Joe turned his attention to one of the bedside tables.

Suddenly Frank asked, "Did you hear something?"

Joe listened intently for a moment, then said, "What did it sound like?"

"Like—"

The hinge on the bedroom door gave a faint squeak.

"Joe," Frank said, in a voice that was eerily calm. "We've got a big problem."

"What's the matter?" Joe demanded, turning.

The door was open wider now. There, in the pool of light from Frank's flashlight, was a gigantic Bengal tiger. It padded slowly toward them, its eyes gleaming yellow in the light. It opened its mouth wide and let out a roar that shook the house.

Chapter

7

THE ROAR OF THE TIGER fixed Frank's feet to the floor. Staying very still, he scanned the room. The tiger was crouched between them and the only exit. But just behind Joe, a partly open door led to the bathroom. It was their best—maybe their only—hope.

"Joe?" Frank said, in a steady voice. "On three, we'll make for the bathroom. One—"

The tiger's ears swung in Frank's direction, and it took another step forward. The tip of its tail twitched.

"Two—"

The huge beast opened its mouth and let out another window-rattling roar, just as Frank shouted, *"Three!"* and dashed for the bathroom door. Joe dove through just in front of him, let him pass, and slammed the door shut.

Joe leaned back against the door, shut his eyes, and took a deep breath. "Why does Helen have a tiger in her house?" he demanded.

"To eat intruders?" Frank suggested. He crossed to the one window and tried to push it open. It was stuck fast. "The main thing is to get out of here before she comes home, finds us, and calls the cops. Chief Collig would love that. Here, give me a hand."

Together, they forced the window up. A chilly breeze blew into the bathroom. Frank put his head out and scanned the area. The ground fell away at this side of the house, but it was still only an eight-foot drop to a soft lawn.

"We can jump easily enough," he told Joe. "But once we're out, there's no way we can shut the window behind us. Helen's going to know someone was here."

There was a loud scratching sound from the other side of the door. "Somebody go let the kitty in," Joe cracked. "Too bad we don't have a bowl of milk to give it."

The window was so small that Frank had to go out head first. As he fell, he did a half somersault and landed on his feet, then fell forward to his hands and knees. A few moments later, Joe hit the ground flat on his back and let out a loud grunt.

"Are you okay?" Frank demanded.

"Just a little winded," Joe replied. He pushed himself up. "Let's move it before Helen comes home and decides to introduce us to her pet."

Joe spent part of Sunday morning in the basement darkroom, while Frank stayed upstairs and studied statistics. He developed the roll of film Frank had shot the evening before and used a hair dryer to dry it quickly. Then he put it in the enlarger. As always, people in the image looked spooky, with all the values of light and dark reversed.

Joe focused the enlarger carefully and made two prints, which he slipped into the tray of developer. Like magic, the latent image slowly appeared. Joe leaned closer and studied it under the dim glow of the red safety lamp. When the prints were fully developed, he picked them up with rubber-tipped tongs and moved them to the tray of fixer, then into the rinsing bath.

As he smoothed the prints onto the heated surface of the print dryer, Joe studied them. They weren't really very good shots. The contrast was weak, and the tiny 8mm negative produced very grainy results when it was enlarged so much. Still, both Helen and Nick were easily recognizable, and so was the apparent relationship between them.

Just as Joe was taking the crisp prints out of

the dryer, the doorbell rang. He grabbed one of them and ran upstairs to answer the door.

It was Vanessa. "Hi," Joe said. "How was soccer this morning?"

"Great," she replied, following him into the living room. "Too bad you didn't come play. I was goalie, and I blocked the shot that would have tied the game. We won three to two."

She wrinkled her nose and added, "Phew. Have you been working in the darkroom?"

"Sorry," Joe said. "I didn't have time to wash my hands before I answered the door."

Vanessa glanced down at the enlargement in his hand. "What's the picture of?" she asked.

Joe handed it to her.

As Vanessa examined the print, her expression hardened. She sat down on the sofa. "Where did you get this?"

"From a picture Helen Papadoulos has in her room," he answered. "We took it last night."

"You saw Helen last night?" Vanessa asked.

Joe hesitated. "Well, not exactly. We went over to see her, but she wasn't there. So we took a look around anyway."

Vanessa frowned. "And you found this," she said. "So now, I bet you think this picture is proof that Helen and Nick are seeing each other. And if she was involved with someone else at the same time that she was engaged to marry Burroughs, you figure she might be the kind of person who'd steal a prize racehorse and set fire to a barn. Right?"

Joe nodded. "Something like that. Of course, it's pretty circumstantial."

"That's for sure," Vanessa said. "All this photo really tells us is that Helen and Nick went sailing once. For all we know, Burroughs is the one who took the picture."

"It's still a clue," Joe insisted.

"I guess so," Vanessa said slowly. "But I think she's innocent. Don't forget, I was with her Friday afternoon. I saw how upset she was about Burroughs dumping her. And I don't believe for a minute that the person I was with had just finished stealing Against All Odds."

"Maybe not," Joe conceded. "But we can't cross her off our list at this point."

"Who else is a suspect?" Vanessa asked. "Nick?"

Joe shook his head. "He's down a few notches. We'd been thinking that he stole Against All Odds to race him under a different name somewhere else, but that wouldn't work. The horse is too well known for that. So there went his motive. Of course, if he really is seeing Helen, he could have done it so that she'd get her half of the insurance money."

"I don't think she'd go for that, either," Vanessa said. "She's not that kind of person."

"So maybe he did it without consulting her,"

Joe said cheerfully. "Anyway, don't forget that he pulled that spear gun on me. That's enough right there to make me suspect him. But we'll know more later. Frank and I are planning to ask Nick a few more questions. Want to come along?"

Vanessa shook her head. "I'd love to, but I promised Chet and Phil that I'd take them riding this afternoon." She stood up and added, "In fact, I'd better run. I've got some homework to do before I meet them at the stables."

After Vanessa left, Joe went upstairs and tapped on the door to Frank's room. Frank was at his desk, still poring over his statistics.

"Ready for a break?" Joe asked. He handed Frank the enlargement. "This might be a good time to swing by Fast Nick's and ask him about this."

Frank checked his watch. "Sure, let's go."

They piled into the van and drove down toward the bay. As they were turning into the marina parking lot, a blue convertible came speeding out, nearly sideswiping them.

"Hey, watch it!" Joe yelled, but the driver was long gone.

"Some people ought to have their driver's licenses revoked," Frank remarked, looking over his shoulder in the direction the car had gone.

"That's for sure," Joe muttered. "But we don't have time to worry about that now."

Joe parked the van near Fast Nick's boat, and the Hardys walked out on the dock. The wind off the water felt chilly and damp. Overhead, the clouds held rain.

When they reached the houseboat, Frank called out, "Permission to come aboard?"

No answer. Frank called again, louder this time, but still there was no answer.

"The gate's open," Joe pointed out. "Maybe he's a late sleeper."

"Let's wake him up, then," Frank replied, striding across the gangplank to the deck.

On board, Joe noted that the folding chair was still where it had been on their last visit. An open book lay on the deck next to it. Joe picked it up. "It's a guide to Portugal," he announced, after studying the cover. "Do you think Nick is planning a vacation in Europe?"

"I think the word you want is *getaway*," Frank replied. "Let's find him and ask."

Joe followed Frank through the doorway into the cabin. At the foot of the short flight of stairs, Frank stopped so abruptly that Joe bumped into him. "Oh, no," Frank said with a groan.

"What's wrong?" Joe demanded.

Frank turned back to his brother. His expression was grim.

"I'm afraid Fast Nick isn't going to Portugal or anywhere else," he said somberly.

Then Frank stepped to one side, letting Joe see the terrible spectacle. Fast Nick lay on the floor in a pool of blood, the harpoon from his spear gun protruding from his chest.

at the top, he
let go and dropped to the deck. Without
a moment to lose, he
ran toward the cabin. He plunged down the
steps to the lighted galley. Nick
lay sprawled on the floor, a spear
gun harpoon buried in his chest.

Chapter

8

FRANK DROPPED TO HIS KNEES beside the jockey
and pressed his fingertips to the side of his neck.
"He's still alive," he told Joe. "Quick, find a
phone. Then look for a first aid kit. I'll do what
I can here."

"Right," Joe said, leaping back up the stairs to
the deck.

Even before Joe was out of sight, Frank had
turned all his attention to Nick. He knew he
shouldn't disturb the harpoon, which would risk
making the injury worse. But he could try to stop
the bleeding. He ripped off his shirt and wadded
it into a ball, then pressed the cloth against Nick's
chest to dam the flow.

Frank spoke to the jockey in a low, calm voice.

"You'll be okay, Nick. Just hold on a few more minutes."

Joe put his head in the doorway and said, "The emergency squad is on its way. I couldn't find a first aid kit anywhere."

"Never mind," Frank said. "Take the blankets off both berths and cover him up. We need to keep him warm until help arrives."

Joe stripped the covers off the double-decker bunk and draped them over Nick. The jockey's face was deathly pale, and his breathing sounded slow and raspy.

Joe tore his eyes from Nick and checked round the cabin. Nothing seemed out of place. "This was no robbery," he said.

"Maybe someone wanted to keep him quiet," Frank said, tending to the wound again.

Joe paced around the cabin. A nylon rope led from the harpoon to the back corner of the room, where the spear gun lay. "Who would want to shut Nick up?" he asked, cutting the rope with his pocketknife. "Helen? Burroughs? Would either of them go this far?"

Frank raised his eyes. "I don't know. But we should do our best to find out before anyone else is hurt. There's the ambulance," he added. "You'd better show them where to come."

Joe dashed upstairs and crossed the gangplank to the dock. The tires screeched as the ambulance pulled up to the main gate. Joe waved both arms over his head and called, "Over here!"

Four emergency medical technicians in blue uniforms piled out of the vehicle and hurried toward him. One carried a big first aid kit, a second had an oxygen tank, and the other two carried a folded-up stretcher.

Joe pointed to Nick's houseboat. "Harpoon in the chest. Heavy bleeding. Straight down the stairs." He followed them onto the boat.

"We'll take over from here," the one in the lead said as they entered the cabin.

"He's all yours," Frank replied, backing up against the wall to give them space. Joe joined him and watched as the emergency squad gave Nick a shot of adrenaline and inserted a plasma and glycerin IV. Working in silence, they lifted Frank's shirt from the wound and applied a sterile dressing.

One of the paramedics, looking at the blood-soaked cloth, said, "You guys saved his life with this."

"You think he'll make it?" Frank asked.

"It's too early to tell, but he's got a chance," the man replied. "We're taking him to Bayport General." With the other paramedics, he lifted Nick onto the stretcher. Frank and Joe followed them on to the deck and watched them load Nick into the back of the ambulance.

"Frank and Joe Hardy," came a familiar voice

from behind them. "I should have known I'd find you here."

"Hello, Chief Collig," Joe said, turning around. "I'm glad to see you."

"I can't say the same," the chief said grumpily. "What happened here?"

Frank said, "We dropped by to talk to Nick, but when we got here, no one answered. We decided to wait on the boat, and we found him in the cabin with a spear in his chest."

"Huh!" Collig said. "The major crime squad will be along in a few minutes, but I want to check it out first."

He walked toward the boat. Frank and Joe followed him. Inside the cabin, he knelt to take a close look at the pool of blood. "How long do you think he'd been lying there before you found him?" he asked the Hardys.

"Not long. Ten minutes max," Frank said.

Chief Collig scratched his chin. "Maybe the wound was self-inflicted," he suggested.

"It wouldn't be easy to shoot yourself with a spear gun," Frank pointed out.

"People have been known to commit suicide with a shotgun or rifle," Collig said. "They can pull the trigger with a toe. Did the victim have his shoes on?"

Joe thought for a moment, then said, "Yes, he did."

Chief Collig pulled out a handkerchief and

picked up the spear gun by the stock. "I wouldn't be surprised if the colonel left his prints all over this," he said, then acted mad at himself for letting the sentence slip out.

"Is Burroughs your top suspect?" Joe asked.

"I didn't say that," Collig said hastily.

"I hear he's trying to collect a million dollars in insurance on Against All Odds," Frank said. "If Nick knew something that would prove the colonel's claim was fraudulent—"

"I know about that," Chief Collig said tersely. "This case is in the hands of experienced police officers. We don't need a couple of amateurs muddying the waters."

"If we hadn't come by when we did," Frank pointed out, "you'd be investigating a murder as well as a horse theft."

"Butt out, kids," the chief growled, "or I'll have to talk to the D.A. about an obstruction of justice charge. Is that clear?"

"Yes, sir," Joe said, careful to keep the sarcasm out of his voice. "Come on, Frank. Let's go see if we can help someone find a lost puppy."

As Joe piloted the van away from the marina, he glanced over and asked, "What do you think, Frank? Any bright ideas?"

"I can think of two reasons for somebody to want to kill Nick," Frank replied. "One, he was an accomplice who was starting to act unreliable.

never been close. He's a good jockey, but
h too hot tempered for my taste."

Were you home this morning, between ten
eleven o'clock?" Frank asked.

Why, no. I spent the weekend with some
nds in New York City. We ate a late breakfast
a restaurant in SoHo, then I drove home. I
n't arrive until about fifteen minutes before
came by. Why?"

"Someone tried to kill Fast Nick this morn-
g," Joe said.

The color drained from Helen's face. For a mo-
nt Joe was sure she was going to faint. Then
e took a deep breath and said, "How is he?
isn't—"

Frank said, "The paramedics arrived quickly.
's got a chance."

"Who could have done such a terrible thing?"
demanded.

Someone who wanted to silence him," Joe re-
l. "Colonel Burroughs, for example."

Brian?" She gave Joe a horrified look. "Brian
dn't kill anybody."

e was a career army officer," Joe pointed
"He's been trained to kill."

a armed enemy, yes," Helen protested.
someone who worked for him for years?
or a dishonorable motive? I know Brian.
er stiff-necked he is, he would *never* com-

Or two, he somehow found out who did it and
the crook had to shut him up."

"What now?" Joe asked.

"Let's check out Helen's place again," Frank
suggested. "Maybe she's home by now."

A station wagon sat in the driveway of the Papadoulos house. Joe parked the van at the curb
and followed Frank to the front door.

Moments after Frank rang the bell, the door
opened.

"Hello," Helen said. "What brings you—"

Her question was interrupted by a deep growl
that Joe recognized instantly. The huge tiger appeared just in back of Helen, staring at Joe and
Frank. Joe couldn't help taking a step backward.

"Gandhi, no!" Helen said in a firm voice.
Then, apparently noticing the expressions on
Joe's and Frank's faces, she added, "Don't worry.
He's pretty harmless. No claws and hardly any
teeth."

She grabbed the tiger by the scruff of the neck.
"Go lie down!" she ordered. The tiger sighed and
padded into the living room, where it curled up
on a rug in front of the fireplace.

"Come in," Helen said, turning back to the
Hardys. "I'm sorry if Gandhi startled you."

"Isn't it dangerous to have a tiger in your
house?" Joe asked.

Helen laughed. "Gandhi is a complete pussy-
cat," she told him. "I borrowed him from a friend

who trains animals for movie work. I'm doing a series of paintings of wild animals."

"We know," Joe said, remembering the canvases he and Frank had seen in her studio.

She gave him a quizzical look. "You do?" she asked. "How do you know that?"

Frank jumped in. "You said something about it at the steeplechase last week. But I don't recall that you mentioned tigers."

"I'm going to have to watch my tongue," she said ruefully. "I was hoping to keep it a secret until the opening of my show in New York next month. Oh, well."

She motioned them to the sofa and sat down facing them. "What can I do for you?"

"You heard about Against All Odds being stolen, didn't you?" Frank asked.

"Yes, it's terrible," Helen replied.

"Well, we're looking into the theft, and we're beginning to think Nick Alexander was involved somehow. But it would have been hard for him to carry it off alone."

As he spoke, Frank watched Helen carefully. Would she betray some telltale sign of guilt?

"If Nick stole the horse," Frank continued, "he would have needed someone to cause a diversion at the auction, so he could set the fire and get away unnoticed. That was quite a scene you made, wasn't it?"

Helen studied his face, then burst out laughing.

"You mean you suspect *me?*" she ⟨...⟩ would I want Brian's horse?"

"We're not accusing you of anythi⟨...⟩ said. "But you do have a reason for ⟨...⟩ get back at the colonel."

Helen sprang to her feet. The tige⟨...⟩ intently. "This is too absurd," she excl⟨...⟩ admit I was upset. I still am. And I c⟨...⟩ that I made a ridiculous scene at the auc⟨...⟩ what does that have to do with stealing ⟨...⟩ horse?"

Joe said, "On Thursday, you told Sam⟨...⟩ stay away from the barn during the ⟨...⟩ Why? Did you know that the barn was ⟨...⟩ catch on fire?"

Helen's voice took on a sharp edge. "⟨...⟩ see that barn *before* it caught fire?" ⟨...⟩ manded. "It was a very hazardous pla⟨...⟩ cially for a small child. When Sam to⟨...⟩ wanted to watch the auction from the⟨...⟩ warned her not to. I would have been ⟨...⟩ ble if I hadn't."

"What is your connection with N⟨...⟩ der?" Joe asked.

"Oh, for heaven's sake!" she bur⟨...⟩ busybody has been gossiping a⟨...⟩ known Nick since high school. I ⟨...⟩ one who introduced him to Br⟨...⟩ while Brian's wife was still alive⟨...⟩

mit a dishonorable act. He'd kill himself first. That's the way he is.

"I'm sorry," she added. "You'd better leave now. I need to be alone. All of this has been a terrible shock."

"What do you think?" Joe asked as he steered the van toward home.

"I believe her," Frank said. "And I believe she's convinced that Burroughs is innocent, too. Of course, she could be wrong."

"Maybe the fire was an accident, after all," Joe speculated. "Though the timing was certainly coincidental. And Odds *is* missing."

As Joe pulled into the driveway, the boys' aunt Gertrude came to the kitchen door. "I'm glad you're home," she said. "I've got some messages for you. First, the hospital called. Someone named Nick Alexander was just operated on and is in stable condition."

"That's great news," Joe said. "What else?"

"Officer Riley called," Aunt Gertrude replied. "He said to tell you that the fire marshal found something called an incendiary timer. So there's no doubt now that someone deliberately set the fire in Colonel Burroughs's barn."

Chapter

9

FRANK AND JOE exchanged a grim glance as they entered the kitchen.

"You boys aren't in any danger, are you?" Aunt Gertrude asked, her voice full of alarm.

"No, no, we're perfectly safe," Frank said quickly. "Is there anything to eat?"

"I can heat up some leftover asparagus and ham casserole," Aunt Gertrude offered.

Joe rolled his eyes. "That's all right, Aunt Gertrude," he said. "We'll take care of ourselves." He opened the refrigerator door and assembled the fixings for turkey subs.

While Joe was making two sandwiches, Frank thought about the message from Con Riley. A timer? That changed the whole case.

"Joe," he said. "That timer—it could have been put in the barn anytime."

Joe nodded, adding a handful of chips to each plate and handing one plate to Frank. "And that means we can't eliminate suspects just because they were at the auction the whole time," he said. "That moves Burroughs up the list, doesn't it? I wonder if Chief Collig is trying to trace the timer."

"Of course. He's a trained professional," Frank quipped. "Wouldn't it be interesting if it turned out to be military hardware?"

"Hurry and eat your sandwich," Joe said. "We've got a date to watch Vanessa teach Chet how to ride a horse."

Frank shook his head. "You'd better go without me. I have to study."

"Okay," Joe said. "But you'll be sorry. This will be better than 'Funny Home Videos.'"

The Lazy R Stables, where Vanessa took riding lessons, was a fifteen-minute drive from town. It was a small outfit with just a dozen horses and a single riding ring, but it backed onto a county park with miles of riding trails.

When Joe arrived, he found Phil and Chet listening to Vanessa explain how to behave around horses.

"How's it going, guys?" Joe said. "Chet? Are you ready to tame this wild beast?"

The wild beast turned its head to give Joe a weary look.

"Sure," Chet said, sounding unconvinced.

"The important thing with horses is to be confident," Vanessa continued. "Comet here is a very experienced saddle horse. If you talk to her in a firm voice, you'll be fine. But if she gets the idea that you're scared of her, she could give you trouble. Any questions?"

"Are you sure he can hold me?" Chet asked.

"Comet's a she, Chet," Vanessa replied. "She'll hold you. You're not that big. Come on, I'll hold the reins while you climb on."

Chet walked slowly toward the horse. "Okay," he said. "Here goes."

"Hey, Chet, catch." Phil threw a small box to his friend. "Put it in your pocket."

"What is it?" Chet asked.

"It's a homing device I built," Phil said. "If Comet runs away, it'll help us find you."

"That won't be necessary," Vanessa said dryly, taking the box from Chet and dropping it in her pocket. "Just remember, Chet. Put your left foot in the stirrup, unless you want to wind up sitting on the horse backward."

Chet stuffed his foot into the stirrup, grabbed the horn of the saddle, and pulled himself up with a groan. Once up he said, "Hey, this is pretty cool."

"Now nudge her with your heels, and she'll start walking," Vanessa told him.

Chet did as he was told. Nothing happened.

"Be nice to her," Vanessa said. "Here you go, Comet."

Comet pretended not to hear.

"Maybe he needs a bigger horse," Phil suggested.

"Come on, Comet," Vanessa coaxed, tugging at the bridle. The horse began to walk slowly forward. But the moment Vanessa released the bridle, it stopped and lowered its head to crop a patch of grass.

After a few minutes Joe got bored. He noticed a big, glossy magazine called *Racing International* in Vanessa's shoulder bag and began to flip through it. After skimming a piece about the first steeplechase in 1752, he started to read an article about racing in Europe.

Apparently, steeplechasing was a hot new fad in Portugal. Officials expected over ten thousand spectators at the Race of Fools on April 1. Most of the entries were well known in Europe, but one, Lightning, was new to the steeplechase circuit. The writer of the article wondered why an inexperienced horse was being allowed to run in such a big race. Next to the article was a photo of Lightning and his owner, a man named Paul Ramika.

Vanessa led Comet back to the stable and helped Chet dismount.

"That was fun," Chet said. "But I think it's enough for one day."

"You must have gone a good thirty feet," Phil cracked.

"Maybe so," Chet replied with great dignity. "But you have to admit that I did every foot of it with *style*."

Frank sat at his desk, doing his best to learn the difference between variance and standard deviation. But all he could think of was Fast Nick, with a spear protruding from his chest. Who had done it? And why?

There was an obvious answer to that last question. Nick must have known something about Odds's disappearance, something that pointed directly to the person who was responsible. Had he tried to blackmail the culprit? Or had he simply let it slip that he knew something? Either way, the guilty party had acted quickly and ruthlessly to silence him.

But that, Frank realized, didn't really answer the question of why. What was it about this theft, and Nick's knowledge, that was important enough to set off a murder attempt? Odds was a valuable horse, but not *that* valuable, especially since, as Nick himself had pointed out, he had no more than another year left to race.

Was it possible that this was one of a series of horse thefts, and that Nick had threatened to reveal the whole plot? There was a way to check on that. Frank put a pencil in his statistics text to mark his place, and moved over to his computer. He booted a communications program and signed on to an on-line data base, then he set up a search on the key subject words *theft* and *horse,* dating from the past ten years.

After five minutes the data base returned the results. Frank let out a groan. During the time period, over one thousand horses were listed as stolen. The only thing worse than no data, he told himself, was too much. The answer he wanted might be right in front of his nose, and he'd never manage to find it in the midst of all the meaningless information. With a disappointed sigh, he logged off.

The phone rang. Aunt Gertrude called from downstairs. "Frank? For you!"

He picked up the receiver.

"Hi, Frank, what's new?" Callie asked.

"More than you'd believe," Frank replied. He told her about finding Nick, and about the fire marshal's discovery. "I thought there might be some kind of link to other horse thefts," he concluded. "But there are just too many of them. When I did a data base search, it turned up over a thousand instances."

"Really?" Callie exclaimed. "That's amazing! I thought horse stealing was something that only happened in Westerns."

"Wa'al, pardner, it just happened right here in Bayport City," Frank drawled.

"Were they all valuable horses, like Odds?" Callie asked.

"Er—I don't know," Frank confessed. "I didn't think about the value of the horses. I guess they couldn't *all* have been very valuable, could they? Most horses aren't."

"Still, all those thefts—wait a minute, Frank," Callie said. "If it hadn't been for you, no one would have ever known that Odds was stolen. Everybody would think that he'd died in the barn fire. Maybe instead of checking on stolen horses, you should be hunting for valuable horses that died accidentally."

Frank's jaw dropped. He took the receiver away from his ear and stared at it. Then he said, "Callie, you're a genius! I'll call back later, after I do a search on horses and accidents. Why didn't *I* think of that!"

He hung up and swiveled his chair to face the computer. He selected the redial menu item and listened as the modem chirped out its signal. Once he was back in the system, he typed in the key words, *horse* and *accident*.

The message, Please Wait, started to blink in the corner of the monitor screen. Frank stood up and began to pace back and forth. At last the computer sent out a faint *beep*.

Frank bent down to look at the screen. Nine

records had come through the search. He sent them to the printer and hovered over it as the printing head zipped back and forth. Finally it was done. He tore off the sheet and scanned it.

All nine records concerned valuable horses that had died accidentally. But six of the nine had something else in common as well. All six had been sold at auction not long before their deaths—and all had been auctioned by Royal Bids, Inc.!

Chapter

10

FRANK TRIED TO THINK through what this meant.
Two thirds of the valuable horses that had died
in accidents in recent years had passed through
the hands of Royal Bids. Could that possibly be
a coincidence? It didn't seem likely. If it wasn't
a coincidence, though, what did it mean?

The obvious possibility was that someone at
Royal Bids was deeply involved in a complicated
horse-stealing racket. If the case of Against All
Odds was typical, the scheme involved replacing
a valuable horse with a stand-in, then arranging
for the stand-in to die in an "accident." As a
result, no one would even know the horse was
still alive, not to mention that it had been stolen.

Frank searched his memory of the auction at

Burroughs's farm. Several members of the auction-house staff had been on hand, from the chief honcho, Philpin, on down. Any of them—or practically anybody else—could have planted the timed incendiary device in the barn. What about the kidnapping of the horse and its replacement by the stand-in? Not so easy to pull off, especially once the public began to assemble for the auction.

Frank heard footsteps coming upstairs. He turned and saw Joe and Vanessa.

"You missed a real treat," Joe said. "The sight of Chet on a horse—"

Frank interrupted him. "Take a look at this." He thrust the printout into Joe's hand. "See anything interesting?"

"Sure," Joe replied after a glance. "Lots of horses have really weird names."

"Here, let me see that," Vanessa said, taking the paper from him. "Hmm—these are all valuable racehorses that suffered accidental deaths. But I don't see where that takes you."

"They were all valuable," Frank pointed out, "but they weren't all racehorses. There were a couple of show jumpers, a hunter, even a champion rodeo cutting horse. But you're right, they all died of unnatural causes."

Frank scanned the printout. "Here's one that was killed on the road when his trailer over-turned. Another broke his leg taking a fence and had to be put down. And here's one in Georgia that was shot by an overeager deer hunter. Nothing so unusual when you take them case by case. But when you look at them all together, a pattern starts to emerge."

"Why isn't Against All Odds on the list?" Vanessa asked.

"He didn't die in the fire," Frank pointed out. "And my guess is that these horses didn't die, either. Do you see anything interesting in the notes area of these reports?"

Joe looked over Vanessa's shoulder. "Frank!" he exclaimed. "Look how many were auctioned by Royal Bids! I think we're onto something here."

"So do I," Vanessa said. "But I don't quite see how you think it would work."

Frank said, "Try this for size. Somebody in the auction firm, or somebody close to the firm, arranges to substitute a run-of-the-mill horse for a champion, then kills off the substitute. Philpin's firm gets its regular commission, so he's happy. The horse's owner gets reimbursed by his insurance company, so *he's* happy. And the horsenapper can sell the real champion for a lot of money."

"That's the part I don't follow," Vanessa said. "If no one knows the horse is a champion, why would it be worth anything at all?"

"Bets," Frank replied. "Say the new owner enters the horse in an important race, under an assumed identity. Everyone will think it's a long shot—everyone but the owner, who knows the horse's real potential. What if he lays out, say, a hundred thousand dollars at fifty to one odds? He could walk away with five million dollars in winnings, not to mention however much the horse earns."

Joe let out a low whistle. Then he took the printout from Vanessa and read over it again. "Why hasn't anybody noticed this, Frank?" he asked. "If two thirds of the horses you auction end up dead, I'd think that people would stop hiring you."

Frank said, "Two thirds of the valuable horses that died accidentally were auctioned by Royal Bids. That doesn't mean that two thirds of the horses Royal Bids auctioned died in accidents. But we can check that directly."

He reached for the Manhattan telephone directory and found the number of Royal Bids, Inc., then dialed it.

"Mr. Philpin, please," he said to the receptionist. He switched on the speakerphone so that Joe and Vanessa could listen in. "Frank Hardy calling."

After a short excerpt of classical music, a man's voice said, "This is Laurence Philpin. What can I do for you, Mr. Hardy?"

"Hello, Mr. Philpin," Frank replied. "I don't

know if you remember me. We met at the auction at Colonel Burroughs's farm."

After a short pause Philpin said, "Of course. You're the kid who saved the little girl."

"No, that was my brother, Joe," Frank told him. "I'm the one who got the horses out. That's what I wanted to talk to you about. We've been asked to investigate the disappearance of Against All Odds, and I'd like to ask you a few questions."

"I'm a very busy man, Frank," Philpin said. "Who hired you to conduct an investigation, anyway?"

Frank hadn't said they'd been hired, but he didn't correct the auctioneer. Vanessa had asked them to investigate, and that was close enough. "That's confidential," he replied.

"Well, I think I can save you a lot of trouble," Philpin said. "In my opinion, the horse was stolen by someone who stood to profit from the insurance. That insurance policy made Against All Odds worth more dead than alive. I'm not accusing anyone in particular, but that's the direction I'd look in if I were you. And I wish you luck. Scandals of this sort are not good for my company's reputation."

Frank pressed on. "What about the other accidental deaths, Mr. Philpin? Did they hurt your company's reputation, too?"

"The silence was longer this time. "Other

deaths?" Philpin finally said in a voice heavy with caution. "What do you mean?"

Frank glanced at the list. "Bustin' Loose in Kentucky, 1987. Away in a Manger in New Jersey and Pass the Buck in Georgia, both in 1990. Beggars Would Ride, 1992. There's a whole list of them, sir. In fact, of the nine valuable horses that have died in accidents in the past few years, six had been recently auctioned by your company. Doesn't that strike you as strange?"

"No, it doesn't," Philpin said coldly. "We are among the world's leading firms in auctioning champion horses. It makes perfect sense that most of any set of valuable horses passed through our hands. And you should be very, very careful about making slanderous accusations. We have a reputation to protect, and we know how to do it."

"I didn't—" Frank began.

Philpin cut him off. "I'm in an important conference right now," he said. "Excuse me."

The line went dead. Frank hung up and looked at his friends. "What do you think?"

Vanessa scratched her head. "Just because Royal Bids auctions a lot of horses doesn't mean they haven't pulled a switch on some of them."

"Let's assume Philpin is guilty and go through it from the beginning," Joe suggested. "Sometime between Odds's visit to the veterinarian and the fire, Philpin swapped horses."

"Or one of his helpers did," Vanessa added.

"Okay, sure," Joe said. "And they could have set the timer in the barn then. Royal Bids keeps a percentage of the sale price and then sells the horse again on the black market. That's a lot of money."

Frank nodded. "And a company like Royal Bids would be in a good position to find a buyer, too. A better position than, say, Helen or Nick. How would amateurs find someone willing to spend that kind of money on a hot horse? And how would they handle payment and delivery? But that's the kind of thing an auction company does every day, without arousing any suspicion."

Vanessa frowned. "There's one problem with the theory, Frank. You're saying the motive is to clean up on bets when the stolen champion races. But racing associations in this country are really careful about preventing that kind of scam. You can't just enter an unknown horse in a big race. He has to have papers and a track record."

"What if you sell the horse to somebody in another country?" Joe asked. "Wouldn't that work?"

"Maybe," Vanessa said. "I don't really know."

"Wait a minute," Frank said. "You two just gave me an idea." He picked up the telephone and began to dial.

"Royal Bids can receive large amounts of money without raising suspicion," he explained.

"But if a sum comes from abroad, and it's over ten thousand dollars, they have to report it to the U.S. Treasury Department. Officer Riley, please," he said into the receiver.

After a short pause, Frank identified himself to Riley, then said, "We got your message about the fire marshal's finding. Thanks for telling us. So it was arson, after all."

"Looks that way," Riley said. "This case is really heating up, and the chief is putting a lot of pressure on us to solve it quickly."

"Maybe we can help," Frank offered. "Do you know anyone with access to international monetary transfer reports?"

"Not directly," Riley said. "But I've got a buddy in the Secret Service. That's part of the Treasury Department, too, you know. He's bound to have the right contacts. Why?"

"You might want to see if a company called Royal Bids has moved any large sums of money into the country recently," Frank said.

"The company that was running that auction at the colonel's place?" Riley said. "I don't see where you're going with this, Frank, but you and Joe have had more than your share of good ideas in the past. I'll check it out and get back to you. But keep it to yourself. If Chief Collig finds out I'm doing this for you, he'll go ballistic on me."

After Frank hung up, Joe said, "I can see a problem with this new theory. Philpin couldn't have spiked Odds's hoof before the race last week. He wouldn't have had any excuse to get near the horse."

"What about earlier?" Vanessa suggested. "Steeplechase horses usually spend one or two nights in the fairgrounds stables before a race."

"Really? Why?" Frank asked.

"They come in from all over the country," she explained. "Because they're moved in open horse trailers, they have to breathe in a lot of exhaust, so they're given some time to get over it."

Joe said, "Could Philpin have sneaked into the fairgrounds the night before the race?"

"There's one way to find out," Frank said.

That night Joe and Frank drove to the fairgrounds and parked behind a clump of trees. The sky was lit by a canopy of stars overhead, the glow of Bayport to the west, and a rising half moon in the east.

Joe glanced at his watch. "Just past midnight," he reported. "We'd better make this quick."

"We sneak in, hang around the stables for a few minutes, then sneak out," Frank replied. "If we can do it, then Philpin could have. Let's go."

Like Joe, Frank was wearing jeans and a dark jacket. Once away from the van, he vanished into the shadows. Joe followed him along the edge of the parking lot, then across the track and toward the stands. They paused in the shelter of the officials' tower.

"Any sign of security?" Frank whispered.

"Not so far," Joe reported. "Which way to the stables?"

"Down to the left, past the paddocks," Frank said. "Come on."

Minutes later they reached the two long, rickety buildings where the horses were stabled before and after races. Now the stalls were empty and silent.

"Okay," Joe said. "We got here. What now?"

As if in answer, a hand reached out of the darkness and clamped onto Joe's shoulder.

"Hey!" Joe whirled around and started to drop into a crouch. Before he could bring his hands up to defend himself, though, a fist slammed into his solar plexus.

"Hungh!" Joe's breath exploded from his lungs and he doubled over, unable to breathe.

Chapter

11

AS JOE SANK to the ground, clutching his middle, Frank took a quick step forward with his left foot and threw a right spinning whip kick over his brother's back. His body came full circle, then *wham!* His heel connected squarely with the cheek of his opponent, a big, meaty guy with gleaming eyes. When the guy didn't go down, Frank followed with an inverted knife-hand to the temple, and the fellow fell heavily.

But it had taken a second or two too long.

Frank sensed another man on his left. Before he could defend himself, the guy rammed his shoulder into Frank's rib cage and drove him back against the stable. A flash of white pain shot through Frank, but the wall behind him kept him upright. He fired off a series of rabbit punches into his attacker's side.

Joe struggled to his feet and started to go to Frank's aid as a third man darted out of the shadows. Joe squared off like a boxer and tagged the new guy with a quick left jab. His opponent answered with a hook-double-uppercut combination that told Joe the guy had been in the ring.

He knew it was time for a quick change in tactics. He cocked his right arm back like an amateur brawler, leaving the left side of his head open for an easy cross. The guy took the bait. Just before his punch connected, Joe dropped his hands and kicked him in the shins. The man went down.

Joe turned to see if Frank needed help, but Frank was standing over his opponent, his hands on his knees as he caught his breath.

"Good job," Joe said, and grabbed the first man who'd attacked him. He pulled him to his feet. "Okay, you," he growled. "I've got a couple of questions to ask before we call the cops."

The man stared at him. "Call the cops?" he said groggily. "You're crazy. We caught you trespassing in the middle of the night. Not to mention beating up security guards."

"Security?" Frank said. Joe heard the concern in his brother's voice. "Aren't you supposed to ask people to leave before you jump them?"

The guy shook his head. "We've got our orders. Any intruders, we grab them and turn them over to the police. The manager clamped down a few months ago after some kids did a job on the place with spray paint. Now we've got about the tightest security around, even when there's nothing going on, like tonight. If there'd been horses here, you bozos wouldn't have even gotten past the fence."

"I'll handle this, Larry," one of the other men said, pushing himself to his feet. "Okay, who are you guys and what are you doing here?"

"Last week before the steeplechase, one of the horses was spiked," Frank said.

"Against All Odds?" the man said. "Yeah, I heard about that. So?"

Joe said, "We were trying to see if the person who did it could have sneaked in the night before."

"Not a chance," the man replied. "It had to be an inside job—the jockey, the trainer, maybe one of the stable hands. Nobody else could have gotten close to that horse."

The third guard said, "I just thought of something, Chuck. The day of the race, I spotted a guy right next to Odds's stall. It looked like he'd been inside and just come out. So I asked him what he was doing, and he flashed a guest-of-owner pass at me and walked away."

"What did he look like?" Joe asked eagerly.

"A big, bald guy, maybe thirty-five," the guard told him.

Frank nodded grimly. That could have been Philpin. Where had he gotten the guest pass? From Colonel Burroughs? Had he given Philpin a pass so that the auctioneer could do the dirty work, while Burroughs stayed in the owners' enclosure and gave himself an alibi?

"Joe?" Frank said. "It's late. We'd better get out of here."

"Hold it," the guard who was in charge said. "You guys are trespassers. We can't just let you walk."

"I'll tell you what," Joe said with grim humor. "You forget you ever saw us, and we won't tell anyone that the two of us got the better of the three of you."

The minute school ended Monday, Frank hurried to the parking lot. Joe was already behind the wheel of the van. He started the engine as Frank settled into the passenger seat and fastened his seat belt. "The colonel's?" he asked.

"Sure thing," Frank replied.

As they neared the farm, Joe said, "Do we try to keep Burroughs from seeing that we suspect him?"

Frank shook his head. "He's sure to guess, whatever we do. And if we let him know we think he's working with Philpin, maybe he'll panic and make a mistake."

Joe drove onto the farm and parked near the house. He and Frank walked up to the front porch. Frank was raising his hand to knock when the door swung open. Burroughs stood there with Samantha on his shoulders. He quickly put her down and said, "Run and play, Sam. Daddy has to talk business."

As Samantha scampered off, Burroughs stepped onto the porch and closed the door behind him. "Well?" he demanded. "What is it this time?"

"Somebody noticed Laurence Philpin around your horse's stall last week before the steeplechase," Frank told him. "When he was confronted, he produced a pass. Did you give it to him?"

The colonel's face reddened. "You fellows aren't still playing Sherlock Holmes, are you? Didn't I tell you to give it up?"

"That's another thing," Joe said. "Why are you so eager to get rid of us? What are you afraid we might find out?"

Burroughs seemed to swell up like a balloon. "Nonsense! You boys are interfering with justice. Let the police do their job. They're the trained professionals, and they don't need help from a couple of bungling kids."

"You know that you're one of their top suspects, don't you?" Frank asked.

"Of course," the colonel said. "In their place, I'd think the same. But as their investigation continues, they'll realize that I'm innocent."

"Did you know Philpin was snooping around the stables before the steeplechase?" Joe asked.

"He wasn't snooping," Burroughs replied. "He'd been trying for months to talk me into retiring Odds and auctioning off the stud rights before it was too late. When I saw him at the race, naturally I offered him a pass."

Frank asked, "Would you have retired the horse if he hadn't stumbled and almost fallen on the home stretch?"

"Maybe not," Burroughs conceded.

"So if Philpin really wanted that commission," Frank continued, "he might have sabotaged the horse to encourage you to sell him. He might have driven a nail into Against All Odds's hoof."

The colonel's face tightened. "You got that from Nick, didn't you? The man will say anything to keep from admitting the obvious. It was his poor riding that caused my horse to almost fall. He was stupid and careless, and it almost cost Odds his life."

"You don't sound very upset about what happened to Nick," Joe remarked.

"Nick ran with a fast crowd," Burroughs replied. "It caught up with him."

"If you don't mind my asking, Colonel," Frank

101

said, "where were you on Sunday morning between ten and noon?"

"I do mind," the colonel said. "You're not an officer of the law, and I don't need to account for my movements to you. But I'll tell you this. I haven't forgotten what I learned during my years of training in unarmed combat. If I had decided to kill Nick, I wouldn't have used a spear gun, and I wouldn't have done a halfway job. He would be dead."

In the tense silence that followed, Burroughs added, "Now, let the police do their job, and get off my property."

"Yes, sir," Frank said. He felt an impulse to salute, but he held it in. Burroughs would certainly take it as a gesture of disrespect and get even angrier.

The Hardys returned to the van and down the long drive. When they reached the main road, Frank said, "Find a place to park where the van can be kind of hidden."

Joe gave him a curious glance, then turned onto the next side road and pulled partway into a grove of trees. "Now what?" he asked.

"I want to check out Burroughs's barn," Frank replied. "Maybe we can find a clue to who torched it."

Frank led the way, cutting through the woods to keep out of sight of the house. They ducked under the ribbons that read Crime Scene Do Not

Cross, and entered the gutted building from the back. The spring breeze had long since blown the smoke away, but the smell of charred wood hung heavily in the air.

"Do you think it's safe in here?" Joe asked.

"Safe enough," Frank said. He pointed to one corner. "See how the burn marks travel up at an angle? I bet that's where the fire started."

As Joe moved closer, he heard an odd squeaking overhead. He glanced up and froze. One of the long, heavy rafters that had once supported the roof was swaying back and forth.

"Frank, we'd better—" Joe started to say.

At that moment one end of the rafter tore loose from the ridge pole. Still attached at the other end, it scythed downward like an executioner's ax. Frank was directly in its path!

Chapter

12

"FRANK, LOOK OUT!" Joe launched himself and grabbed his brother in a flying tackle. The two of them crashed to the ash-covered floor and rolled. The huge rafter came swinging down and knifed the spot where Frank had been standing. Specks of charred wood came raining down.

"We'd better get out of here," Frank said. "The colonel might come out to see what happened."

Joe stood up and grinned at Frank, who was coated in black dust from head to toe. "You look like the chimney sweep in *Mary Poppins*," Joe told him.

"Talk about the pot calling the kettle black," Frank replied. He brushed some of the ashes off, then headed for the door.

"Frank, check this out," Joe said.

Frank turned back. A nail protruded from a wooden post that had not been touched by the fire. A small piece of green cloth had snagged on it. Frank bent over to examine it. "Good work, Joe. If we find someone with a torn jacket that matches this, it's evidence they were in the barn at some point."

"That doesn't mean they torched it," Joe said.

Frank carefully removed the scrap of cloth and slipped it into his wallet. "No, but it's a start," he replied. "Now to get back to the van without the colonel spotting us."

The Hardys were nearing the outskirts of Bayport when Joe glanced in his rearview mirror. A gray sedan was driving too close to their rear bumper. "Get off my tail," Joe muttered.

In the next second Joe thought the guy in back was going to ram them. He sped up, and the gray car sped out into the left lane and pulled up alongside them. The tinted window lowered, and Joe saw the barrel of an automatic weapon appear.

"Down!" he shouted to Frank. He slid down in his seat, floored the gas pedal, and swung the wheel to the left, hoping the threat of being sideswiped would throw the gunman off balance.

The burst of fire sounded like a continuous roar. The side window next to Joe shattered. A split second later the windshield became a cloudy white spider web, then fell inward in a million tiny pellets. Joe slammed on the brakes. "Frank! Are you all right?" he gasped.

Frank sat up and tried to brush the pellets of glass off. "I'm not hurt," he said. "But they're getting away. Let's go after them."

The sedan was almost out of sight. "They've got a lead on us," Joe said, "but maybe we'll get lucky."

Their attackers must have assumed that Joe and Frank were out for the count and hoped to avoid notice by driving slowly. The moment they spotted the Hardys' van approaching, they took off.

"Gun," Frank warned. Joe kept his head low and weaved back and forth as the automatic appeared out the sedan's front passenger window and fired off several short bursts. This time the slugs missed.

"Deadman's Curve is just ahead, on the other side of this hill," Frank warned.

"I know," Joe said. "But I don't think those guys do." He pushed the van even harder as they started up the incline. The moment the sedan went over the crest of the hill, he began to slow. A moment later he heard a tremendous crash.

"You were right," Frank said grimly. "They didn't know about it. I'll call the cops," he added, picking up the cellular phone.

Joe stopped the van at the crest of the hill. From there, the road descended steeply, then made a sharp bend to the left. The gray sedan had skidded off and finished right side up against a tree.

Joe parked on the shoulder, and he and Frank cautiously approached the car. The two occupants were slumped down, eyes closed. Were the gunmen playing possum, waiting until Joe and Frank got close enough for them to finish the job? Trying to ignore the smell of spilled gasoline, Joe forced open the driver's door.

"They're both alive," he told Frank. "I can see the gun on the floor."

Frank helped him pull the driver from the car. While Frank dragged the first man a safe distance away, Joe took care of the gunman, who was teetering on the edge of consciousness. Frank returned to retrieve the gun. It was a black machine pistol with what looked like a twenty-five-round clip. Frank pulled out the clip, then snapped the arming lever to make sure there wasn't a live round in the chamber.

A scuffling noise alerted Joe. He turned, just as the gunman pushed himself to his feet and started toward the van.

"In your dreams, yo-yo," Joe growled, and dashed after him. He grabbed the gunman's shoulder, spun him around, and gave him a hard left to the neck. The gunman staggered backward and slumped to the ground.

"Okay, you," Joe said. "Why did you try to kill us?"

The gunman sat up, rubbing his neck, and stared warily at Joe. "I didn't," he said. "All we were trying to do was scare you."

"Then why the pistol?" Joe demanded. "Why didn't you just sneak up and scream, 'Boo'?"

"Come on," Frank added. "Who put you up to this?"

The guy shook his head. "I don't know. A voice over the phone—a thou up front and the rest when we finished the job. The usual."

Joe heard sirens in the distance. "That's all you can tell us?" he asked. "Last chance."

"That's all I know," the man said.

Two cruisers swooped down the hill and screeched to a stop. The officers jumped out and spread out, their guns in a two-handed grip.

"Freeze!" one of them shouted. "Nobody move."

"Those kids are all right," another voice said. Joe was relieved to recognize this voice as Con Riley's.

Riley came down the embankment toward them. "What's the story here?" he asked, looking from the Hardys to the gunman and the driver, who was just beginning to stir. His eyes widened. "Do you know who you were dealing with?"

Frank shook his head and said. "Not a clue." Riley quickly handcuffed the driver, then covered the gunman while one of the other officers cuffed him.

"Meet Cliff Mason and Dirk Viper," Riley said. "We had a fax from the FBI about them just a couple of weeks ago. They're professional hit men, wanted for murder in a couple of states.

"Garret," he added, turning to one of the other officers. "Put the two perps in the back of the cruiser and wait for me. I'll take a statement from these two."

"Right," Garret said.

Riley waited until the others were out of earshot. Then he said, "Boys, you'd better watch yourselves. If somebody cares enough to bring in professional hit men, there must be a lot more to this than one stolen horse. And that means you're in a lot of danger."

"That's both good and bad news," Frank said.

"What do you mean?" Riley asked.

"It's bad news because we're going to have to be a lot more careful," Frank told him. "But it's also good, because it proves we're getting close enough to spook the bad guys."

"Just watch yourselves," Riley repeated. "Oh—I talked to my buddy in Treasury. Royal Bids must have a lot of foreign customers, because they file International Monetary Transfer forms pretty regularly. In fact, just last week they received a quarter-million-dollar transfer from Lisbon. Does that help at all?"

"I don't know," Frank told him. "But thanks anyway."

"Now." Officer Riley took his notebook from his hip pocket. "What happened here?"

The Hardys made their statements and promised to come by headquarters the next day to sign them. Then they climbed into the van.

"The statements are a formality," Riley assured them, leaning in through the shattered window. "These dudes are facing murder raps."

As Joe started the engine, Frank said, "Let's get home. With luck, I can put in another half hour on statistics."

The driveway at the Hardy house was empty. Joe parked the van in its usual spot, then he and Frank went inside. Joe spotted the red light blinking on the answering machine and pressed the playback button.

"Frank? Joe? Are you there? This is Helen Papadoulos." The voice filled the room with a sense of panic. Frank and Joe exchanged worried glances as the voice continued. "Please, call me back as soon as you get this message. I need help right away. Call me, *please!*"

Chapter

13

As THE SOUND of Helen's terrified voice died away, Joe lunged for the phone. "What's her number?" he demanded. "She didn't leave it on the machine."

Frank pulled out the local area phone book, flipped through it, and gave Joe the number.

Joe dialed. The phone rang four times before Helen picked it up and said, "Hello?" Her voice quavered.

"Helen, this is Joe Hardy," he said. "Are you all right?"

"Joe!" she cried so loud he had to pull the receiver away from his ear. "Thank goodness you called. I didn't know where to turn. You and your brother must help me!"

"Take it easy," Joe urged. "Calm down and try to tell me what's the matter."

"How can I calm down!" Helen cried. "They're going to arrest Brian. You've got to stop them."

"Who's going to arrest him?" Joe asked.

"Why—the police, of course," she stammered. "They think he stole Against All Odds to get the insurance money."

Something about this didn't sound right to Joe. How could Collig have enough evidence to arrest Burroughs? Had the two hit men confessed that the colonel had hired them? That didn't make sense. Even if their story about being hired through an anonymous phone call was false, professional criminals didn't usually cave in that quickly.

"Helen?" Joe said in a soothing voice. "What exactly did you hear? That Chief Collig *wanted* to arrest Colonel Burroughs or that he was *planning* to arrest him?"

"Well, neither," she admitted. "But he did say that Brian was his top suspect."

Joe rolled his eyes. "Okay, then," he said. "Chief Collig's someone who always goes by the book. Unless he's sure the colonel is guilty and can prove it, he won't make an arrest. I don't think you have to worry."

"Oh, I hope you're right," Helen said, a hint of a sob in her voice. "Brian is such a wonderful man, and I really love him. We were so happy before he had his attack of jealousy. What on earth am I going to do?"

"Have you tried talking to him?" Joe asked.

"What could I say?" she replied.

"Just tell him what you've told me," Joe suggested. "It can't hurt."

She paused, and Joe could hear her blowing her nose. "I'll give it a try."

"Why not?" he said.

"Oh, Joe, thank you so much," she said. "You've been so wonderfully helpful. I don't know what I would have done without you."

Joe replaced the receiver. "One more emergency handled with care," he said to Frank.

"Joe Hardy, advisor to the lovelorn," Frank said with a grin.

Joe grabbed a pillow off the sofa and threw it at him.

The moment the Hardys got home from school the next day, Frank vanished into his room with his statistics textbook. A little later Callie and Vanessa dropped by with Phil and Chet.

"Frank's upstairs studying," Joe told Callie. "He threatened to drop boiling oil on anybody who interrupted him."

"Oh?" Callie responded. "We'll see about that."

While Joe led the rest of the gang down to the

basement, Callie climbed the stairs and knocked on Frank's door. Joe heard Frank's shout of "Go away!" from the other end of the house. He met Vanessa's eye and winked.

Five minutes later Callie reappeared with Frank. "Tah-dah!" she said, stepping aside and gesturing toward him.

"Frank! Joe said you'd bricked yourself up in the wall," Chet said.

"Almost," Frank said. "Anybody want to ask me a question about correlation coefficients?"

"Sure, what are they?" Phil asked.

A fixed look came over Frank's face. "The Pearson product-moment correlation coefficient," he began, in a voice that sounded computer-generated, "is the most widely used measure of—"

"Cut!" Joe said. "That's as much as Phil really wanted to know."

"Joe was telling us about the attack on you yesterday," Vanessa said. "That must have been really scary."

"Who do you think hired those thugs?" Chet asked.

Frank dropped sideways into an easy chair and draped his legs over the arm. "Fast Nick is still in the hospital, so he's in the clear."

"It could have been Burroughs," Joe said, avoiding Vanessa's eye. "He made it clear he wants us off the case."

"Helen's not the kind of person who'd fall in love with a murderer," Vanessa said flatly.

"How many people are?" Joe retorted.

"Then there's Philpin," Frank said. He told the others about what he'd found through his data base search. "I let Philpin know what we suspected," he concluded. "Maybe, in light of what happened with those two hoods, that wasn't such a shrewd move."

"Trying to have someone blown away seems like a pretty extreme reaction," Phil said. "Is the theft of this horse really *that* big a deal?"

"We don't really know," Frank said. "And we don't know how it ties in with the rest of Philpin's operation. For instance, he got a payment of hundreds of thousands of dollars the other day from Portugal. Legitimate or not? We don't really know," he repeated.

Joe frowned. Something was tickling the back of his mind. "Wait a second, Frank," he said. "What did you just say? Was it—Portugal! Right!"

Joe turned to a startled Vanessa. "Vanessa, do you still have that copy of *Racing International* that I was looking at the other day?" he demanded.

"Why—I guess so," she replied. She looked through her bookbag and pulled out a glossy magazine. "Why do you want it?"

"Great," Joe said. He took the magazine and

began flipping the pages, starting at the back. Where was the article he had skimmed while Chet was trying to learn to ride? "Okay, listen to this." He began to read aloud.

" 'Steeplechasing: Sport of the Decade in Portugal. April first marks the third running of the Race of Fools, the largest steeplechase in Portugal. With more than ten thousand observers and a purse of one hundred thousand dollars, this is one more sign that steeplechasing is becoming one of Portugal's most popular pastimes.' "

He turned the page and began skimming. "Blah, blah, blah. Okay, here. 'A top attraction is veteran trainer Paul Ramika's new stallion, Lightning.' " He held out the magazine to his friends. "Check out the picture of Lightning in the lower left-hand corner."

Vanessa stared at the photo of a gray stallion with a jagged white streak down his nose. "Joe!" she exclaimed. "That could be the twin to Against All Odds. But how—"

Frank took the magazine and read, then shook his head. "It doesn't hang together," he said. "Odds has been missing for less than a week. He couldn't be in Portugal already. And anyway, this magazine must have gone to press a month ago or more. That can't be our horse."

"Why do you think the picture was taken in Portugal?" Callie asked. "It could have been taken last year, then recently sent to the magazine."

Frank stared at the ceiling. "It's possible," he said. "But if you had just spent a lot of money for a stolen horse, with the idea of cleaning up in a scam, would you send a picture of the horse to a widely circulated magazine first? Of course not."

Phil said, "Maybe the journalist got his information straight from the race authorities and published it without asking the owner. That would certainly make the bad guys nervous."

"Nervous enough to try to kill Joe and me over a phone call?" Frank asked.

"Maybe," Phil said. "If the stakes are high enough."

"Wait. We can find out if that's Against All Odds," Vanessa said excitedly. She snatched the magazine out of Frank's hands. "Let's go to my place and scan it into the computer. We can do an image comparison against the real Against All Odds and see if it is the same horse."

"Can you do that?" Chet asked as everyone stood up.

"Vanessa can do anything she wants with computers," Joe bragged.

They were on their way to the van when Chet remembered that he had promised to be home for a phone call.

"I'll drive you," Phil said. "But listen, you guys. We'll expect a full report tomorrow."

"You'll get it," Frank promised as he, Joe, and the two girls piled into the newly repaired van for the drive.

Vanessa lived with her mom, also a computer graphics whiz, in an old farmhouse. Joe pulled up in the drive, then he, Frank, and Callie followed Vanessa up the path and through the back door.

"Hi, Mom," Vanessa said.

"Hello, Ms. Bender," the others said in ragged unison.

"Hi, everybody. Did you find that horse yet?" Ms. Bender asked with a wry smile.

"Not yet," Vanessa said. "We're headed upstairs to play with the computer. Call if you need me to help with anything."

"I will," her mother replied. "We'll be eating at six-thirty."

As usual, Vanessa's room was littered with notebooks, computer manuals, stuffed animals, and art supplies. A piece of plywood spanned two low file cabinets to form a computer table. Vanessa marched over and hit the Resume button on her keyboard. Multicolored winged fish began to swim across the large-screen monitor.

"Okay, where's the magazine?" she asked.

Joe opened it to the right page and handed it to her. She placed it facedown on top of the scanner and pressed a button on the side. Line by line, the photograph from the magazine appeared on the screen. Vanessa tapped several keys. The photo expanded until it filled the left half of the display.

"Is that Against All Odds?" Frank asked.

"We'll see in a few minutes." Vanessa pulled down a communications menu and made a series of choices. The telephone started beeping. "I'm dialing into the National Steeplechase Federation's data base," she explained. "They keep computer images of every horse that's registered with the organization. All I have to do is download the one of Odds, then compare it to this one."

A picture of Against All Odds appeared on the right side of the screen. Joe groaned. "This is hopeless," he said. "That's a profile and the one out of the magazine is at an angle. How can you compare them?"

"Easy," Vanessa replied. She used the mouse to pull down a different menu and clicked on one of the items. A dial popped up in the bottom corner of the screen. She rotated the arrow on the dial to twenty degrees, then pressed the OK button. As if guided by an invisible hand, the image of Against All Odds rotated to the position of the other shot.

"The Steeplechase Federation keeps digitized images in three-D," she said. "Watch." With the mouse, she dragged the left image over the right until they lined up. Then she selected the Compare menu option. The disk access light on the computer began to blink in an irregular pattern.

"What's it doing now?" Joe asked.

Vanessa said, "The computer's measuring the distance between key points on the two images. If the variation is less than fifteen or twenty percent, there's reason to suspect a match."

The teens watched. To Joe, the time seemed endless, but finally the computer let out a plaintive *beep*. Vanessa typed another command. A new line of type appeared at the bottom of the screen. Points of Similarity 97%, it read.

"There's your answer," Vanessa said, in a voice that throbbed with excitement.

Chapter

14

"THERE'S YOUR PROOF," Vanessa exclaimed, pointing to the computer screen. "Lightning *is* Against All Odds."

She grabbed the telephone receiver and handed it to Joe. "Here, call the police and tell them what we've discovered."

"Not so fast," Joe said, placing the telephone back in the cradle. "We can't go to the police without solid evidence."

"We have a ninety-seven percent match," Vanessa said. "We found Against All Odds. Isn't that enough?"

"Not for the cops," Joe told her. "They want witnesses, facts, not two photos that overlap."

"Still," Frank said thoughtfully, "we're building a strong case against Philpin. The security guards saw him near Odds's stall before the race. He had the best chance to steal the horse, after taking it to the vet. His company just received a large payment from Portugal. And Odds is apparently registered to race there under a different name." He shook his head. "If only we had one solid witness."

"What about Fast Nick?" Joe said. "If he's in any shape to talk, maybe he'll tell us who shot him with the spear gun. I bet it's the same person who stole Against All Odds."

"I'll call the hospital," Callie volunteered, reaching for the phone. When she hung up, she reported, "He's conscious but on medication and may not be able to talk. Also, visiting hours end in fifteen minutes."

"What are we waiting for?" Frank demanded, striding toward the door.

"I don't believe this." Joe pounded the steering wheel. Half a block ahead a huge moving van was making its third attempt to back into a narrow alley. In the meantime it had blocked all traffic behind it on the street.

"We'll never get to the hospital in time." Frank glanced at the dashboard clock.

"I'm going around the other way," Joe announced. He backed up to make a U-turn, then hurried to the intersection and turned right.

Three minutes later Bayport General Hospital came in sight. Joe found a parking spot and the four teens hurried inside.

"Visiting hours are nearly over," the nurse on Nick's floor told them.

"Oh, no!" Callie said, arranging her face in a look of distress. "We came all the way here to see Nick Alexander."

"I'm sorry," the nurse said.

"But these are the guys who saved Nick's life," Vanessa added. "Just a few minutes?"

The nurse softened. "Well, all right, but don't stay long."

"We won't," Frank promised and started down the corridor to Nick's room. The jockey was lying on his back with his eyes closed. Two IVs dripped medicine into his arm, and a clear plastic tube led into one nostril.

"Nick? How are you feeling?" Frank asked.

Nick opened his eyes and turned them toward Frank's face. Otherwise, he didn't move.

"Nick, we're trying to nail the person who shot you," Joe said. "But we need help."

There was no reaction. Frank wondered if this visit was pointless. In the shape Nick was in, how could he identify his attacker?

"Nick," Frank said. "If you can hear me, blink your eyes twice."

Very slowly the jockey's eyelids closed and opened two times.

"Great," Frank said. "Now, first, some good news. We think we've figured out who stole Odds and why. If we're right, it's the same guy who tried to kill you. I'll say his name, and if I'm right, blink twice. Is it the president of Royal Bids, Laurence Philpin?"

Nick's eyes darted frantically from right to left. Then he blinked two times.

Frank squeezed the jockey's hand. "That's what we needed to know. We'll call the police and they'll put out a warrant for his arrest." He stood up, but Nick didn't release his grip. He held on even tighter.

"I think he wants to tell us something else," Vanessa said.

Nick blinked twice.

"Try this," Callie said, taking a pad and pencil out of her coat pocket. She put the pencil in Nick's hand and held the pad where he could reach it. The jockey struggled to scratch out the letters P LEAVING US.

"Leaving us?" Frank read. "I don't—"

Nick blinked once then stared imploringly from one to another of his visitors.

"Leaving the U.S.? Philpin's planning to leave the country?" Joe asked. Relief washed over the jockey's face, and he blinked twice. "Soon?" Joe pursued. The jockey blinked twice, then twice again for emphasis.

"We don't have time to fool around with Chief

Collig and a warrant," Frank said grimly. "We'll have to get him ourselves."

On the drive into New York City, Joe, Frank, Callie, and Vanessa talked over ideas of how to smoke out the crooked auctioneer. Though rush hour had begun, the heaviest traffic was coming out of the city, so Joe was able to make good time.

Royal Bids occupied a small building near the Holland Tunnel. Joe parked down the block, then got out to survey the situation. He returned to the van excited.

"See that blue convertible parked across the street?" he said. "That's Philpin's."

"How do you know?" Vanessa asked.

"That's the car that nearly sideswiped us at the marina the other day, right before we found Nick," Joe explained. "One more piece of evidence against Philpin."

Frank nodded. "Okay, gang, let's do it," he said. "Ready, Callie?"

Callie gave him a nervous smile and picked up the car phone's receiver. Frank dialed Philpin's number. He held his breath until Callie gave him a thumbs-up. Someone was still in the office.

Callie took a deep breath and said, "Senhor Philpin if you please. I am Patricia da Silva of the Consulate of Portugal."

Joe caught Frank's eye and grinned. Callie's

accent sounded more Spanish than Portuguese, but he doubted that Philpin's receptionist, or Philpin himself, would notice the difference.

After a pause, Callie identified herself again and said, "We are having confusion at the consulate regarding an import form from a Senhor Paul Ramika. Is this a name you know?"

They had decided in advance that Callie should name the man they suspected of buying Odds, to tighten the screws on Philpin. It worked. When Callie held the receiver a little away from her ear, Joe could hear Philpin stuttering, "No, I— That's not a name I know."

"This is very unusual, Senhor," Callie continued. "I was in the hope that we might avoid a full investigation, but now ..." She let her voice trail off.

"Anything I can do to help," Philpin said quickly. "What's the problem?"

Frank patted Callie's shoulder and Joe made a circle with his thumb and forefinger. She was handling this like a champ. She grinned at them and said, "Perhaps it would be better to discuss this with an investigator."

Philpin began to sound nervous. "Um—that would be fine, of course. But if you told me what the problem is, perhaps we could save everyone a little inconvenience."

Frank scribbled "Use the name Lightning" on a notepad. Callie nodded, then said, "Senhor

Ramika has filed for permission to import a race-horse named Lightning into Portugal. On the form he said Royal Bids was the breeder. However, you have not filed an affidavit of animal expatriation. We have very strict rules of quarantine, you know."

Philpin interrupted. "Mrs. da Silva, this is a large company. I can't possibly keep my eye on every minuscule transaction. Why don't I look into this and call you tomorrow?"

Callie smiled, hearing the panic in his voice. "I'm afraid this must be cleared up sooner than that. The authorities in Lisbon have demanded an immediate response. Someone from the consulate will be at your office shortly. Good afternoon." Then she hung up.

"All right!" Vanessa cried.

"Great job, Callie," Frank said.

"He sounded awfully nervous," Joe added. "If our plan works, he should be coming out the door in a couple of minutes. Are you ready?"

Callie held up Phil's homing device and nodded, then stepped out of the van and started down the sidewalk toward the Royal Bids building. Joe knew she didn't like the idea of making contact with the man who may have tried to kill Fast Nick, but she was the only one of them Philpin had never seen. There was no chance he'd recognize her.

As Callie approached the building, Laurence

Philpin hurried out. He had a trench coat slung over his arm and a bulging briefcase in his right hand. As if by accident, Callie cannoned into him, knocking the briefcase to the ground. Files spilled onto the sidewalk.

Joe watched Callie mouthed apologies as she bent down to help put the files back into the briefcase. He didn't see her tuck the homing device inside, and obviously the crooked auctioneer didn't, either.

Philpin brushed Callie aside and hurried across the street to the blue convertible. A moment later he drove away.

Callie waited until he was at the next block, then ran back to the van and jumped in. The moment the door closed, Joe pulled away from the curb and followed the convertible.

"There he is," Frank said, pointing up ahead. "I think he's heading for the tunnel."

"Think we can keep up?" Callie asked.

Frank opened a panel on the dashboard to reveal a small video screen, then pressed a switch at the top. The screen began to glow, and a dot flickered slightly above center.

"If Phil's homing device works as it's supposed to," he said, "we should be in good shape, especially at close range. But all these buildings can confuse the signals. We don't want to get too far behind."

"And keeping up with him's my job," Joe said,

pulling around a double-parked delivery van. He glanced around to give Vanessa a grin.

"Joe, look out!" she screamed.

Joe whipped his head around. Hidden by the delivery van, a gigantic garbage truck was pulling out of a loading dock right in front of him.

"Hold on," Joe shouted. "We're going to crash!"

Chapter

15

THE INSTANT JOE SAW the huge garbage truck looming up on his right, he turned the wheel sharply to the left and slammed on the brakes. The van started to skid sideways, then scraped its right side along the massive front bumper of the truck. It all seemed to happen in slow motion, and Joe found time to remember the scene from a movie in which the *Titanic* sailed past the fatal iceberg, slitting open its hull as it went. Then they were past the garbage truck. Joe tried to correct the spin, but before he could regain control, the van's wheels hit the opposite curb. Shaken, Joe brought the vehicle to a stop.

"Everybody all right?" Joe asked. Frank gave a short nod and turned around. Vanessa and Callie were both pale, but unhurt.

"What do we do now?" Vanessa asked. "Philpin is getting away."

"Leaving the scene of an accident is a crime," Joe reminded her. He switched off the engine. "We'll just have to keep our fingers crossed and hope that the tracker works the way it's supposed to."

"You guys stay in the car," he added. "I'll make this as quick as I can."

Joe waited for a car to pass, then crossed to the driver's side of the garbage truck. The driver, a big guy with round cheeks, wore a windbreaker with the words *Hercules Haulers* embroidered on the chest and a faded Mets cap. "Buddy, you're lucky I didn't flatten you," he said to Joe. "Don't you ever watch where you're going?"

"You were hidden by that double-parked delivery truck," Joe retorted. "Are you okay?"

"I'm fine, but the side of your van is a mess," the man said.

Joe suggested, "Since nobody was hurt, why don't we save each other a lot of hassle and drive on off?"

"Can't be done," the man replied. "My boss is really strict about that. We'll have to wait for the cops."

At that moment a police car came along and stopped. The two officers listened to Joe's account and filled out the accident report. The process took no more than fifteen minutes, but for

Joe it felt like hours. Where was Philpin now? Boarding a plane for Portugal with his illegal millions?

Joe hurried back to the van and started the engine. "Is the homing device still tracking?" he asked.

Frank shook his head. "The light has been blinking at the bottom of the screen for ten minutes or so. Philpin's out of range."

"What do we do?" Vanessa wailed. "He's going to escape with Against All Odds."

Frank said, "I say we go through the tunnel to New Jersey and head for the turnpike. In more open countryside, this gadget has a lot more range. Maybe we'll pick him up again."

"Why New Jersey?" Callie asked. "He could be headed upstate or even to Connecticut."

"True," Frank said. "But he chose to locate his company near the Holland Tunnel, and his car had Jersey plates. It's not a sure thing, but does anybody have a better idea?"

Joe shrugged. "Let's roll."

Once through the tunnel, Joe took the Pulaski Skyway, an elevated road that looked like something from an Erector Set manual. "The higher we are, the more range we'll have," he explained. "Besides, I like the view of the Jersey Meadows from up here."

"I always knew you were a little strange,"

Vanessa cracked, staring out at the marshes that seemed to stretch for miles.

They were nearing the Turnpike entrance when Frank suddenly said, "Contact! He's about ten miles south-southwest of us." He pulled a map from the door pocket and studied it, then added, "Head for the Oranges, Joe."

"You got it," Joe replied with a grin.

A quarter hour later he left the highway and, following Frank's instructions, took a suburban street that gradually became more rural. Soon there were fields and woods on either side. Just as they passed a turnoff with a small wooden sign for the Shady Rest Stables, the locator let out a beep.

"There!" Frank said. "Take that turn."

Joe turned left onto a narrow gravel road that led through woods so thick that he turned on the headlights. At the end of the road was a small, clapboard farmhouse with a long whitewashed stable building behind it. Philpin's blue convertible was parked in front.

"Bingo," Joe said as he climbed out of the van. He ran up to the porch and banged on the front door, but there was no answer. "He's here somewhere. Come on, let's look around."

Frank, Callie, and Vanessa stepped out of the van. "Check this out," Vanessa said, pointing to a single tire track in the mud.

"That looks like a pretty big bike," Frank said. "Let's see where it went."

The four teens walked down a small trail, following the tire marks. Fifty yards from the house, they came to a forestry gate—a pipe three inches thick mounted across the track to keep cars out. Someone had left it open.

Past the gate, the woods were even thicker. "I see why he didn't bring his car up here," Callie said.

"Yeah," Frank replied. "This is definitely four-wheel-drive territory."

As they walked around a tight bend, Frank heard the low rumble of an engine. What could that be? Moments later, as the trail emerged into a small clearing, he got his answer.

Laurence Philpin sat behind the wheel of a small bulldozer, backing it out of a pit that was obviously freshly dug. Just then, the dusk was lit by a flash of lightning. After the clap of thunder, a horse whinnied loudly.

Frank looked around. At the edge of the clearing, a big black horse was tethered to a tree, pawing the ground nervously. Parked near it was a big motorcycle.

Frank suddenly realized Philpin's latest scheme. He was going to shoot Against All Odds and bury him where no one would ever find him, then flee the country.

Vanessa seemed to understand in the same instant. "Oh, no, he can't!" she wailed. She ran along the edge of the clearing to the horse, then stroked its nose and spoke to it in low, comforting tones. To Frank's surprise, she reached into her pocket and pulled out a sugar cube. The horse gobbled it down.

"Forget it, Philpin," Joe suddenly called. "It's all over."

Philpin peered over his shoulder in surprise. The bulldozer's engine fell silent. "What are you doing here?" he shouted, climbing down from his seat and walking toward them. "This is private property. Get out, before I call the police."

"The police?" Frank said with a snort. "Good idea. I'll even lend you the quarter."

Philpin lit a cigarette and took a nervous puff. He didn't even notice when he dropped his lighter. "I know you," he said aggressively. "You're the ones who called me the other day with a bunch of wild accusations."

"Not so wild," Joe said. "We found Against All Odds, didn't we? And just in time, too."

"Did you really think you could plant a bullet in Odds's head and bury him here without anyone getting wind of it?" Frank added.

"You must be color blind," Philpin growled. "Against All Odds, wherever he is, is a gray horse with white markings. This horse is as black as coal. I've got to put him down. He's got hoof and mouth disease. If I don't destroy him, he'll infect every horse in the county."

Vanessa pressed her thumbs against the horse's lips and inspected the gums. They were pink and healthy. "Odds looks fine to me."

"Listen, girl. That isn't Against All Odds. Check the tattoo on the inside of his hip. It's not Burroughs's horse."

Frank scooped Philpin's lighter up off the ground and walked over to the horse. "You can change a horse's color, and even a tattoo," he said. "But there are some things you can't change."

He held the lighter beside the horse's head and flicked it on. The horse showed no reaction. "You can't fake tunnel vision," Frank said. "This horse is Against All Odds."

"It was a clever plan," Joe said. "You knew a man in Portugal who wanted a champion horse to run in the Race of Fools. Odds would almost certainly win the hundred-thousand-dollar purse."

"Do you think it would be worth someone's time to steal a horse for a hundred thousand dollars?" Philpin countered.

"That's only the beginning," Frank pointed out. "Because no one would know who he is, the owner could win huge bets on the side. Plus, he could race him in other steeplechases in Europe. Under a different name a champion race horse is worth millions. Only Burroughs didn't want to sell. You made a promise you couldn't keep."

"But you found a good way to change the colonel's mind," Joe said, taking up the story. "He invited you to the race, and you arrived early. When everyone was worried about registering the horse, you sneaked into the stable and spiked Odds's hoof."

"You could have killed him!" Vanessa said.

"If that had happened," Frank deduced, "then you wouldn't have made the sale. But you wouldn't have gotten in trouble with the buyer. If Against All Odds was dead, you might have stolen a different horse in a couple of months."

"Your gamble paid off," Joe said. "Burroughs agreed to auction the horse. Then you took Odds to the vet. After getting him checked out, you swapped Odds for a run-of-the-mill stallion, dyed to look like the champion. To make sure no one found out, you set fire to the barn to destroy the evidence."

Philpin remained calm, far too calm for someone who'd been caught red-handed. Frank began to worry what he might have up his sleeve. The auctioneer shrugged. "How could I have set that fire? I was running the auction."

"The fire marshal found what was left of the timer," Frank told him. "You planted the bomb before the auction."

Philpin reached under his jacket and pulled out

a black machine pistol. "You kids are pretty smart," he said. "But there's one thing you didn't notice. That trench over there is plenty big enough for a horse *and* you four. And without you, there isn't a scrap of evidence against me. Sorry to end our discussion so soon," he added, leveling the weapon.

"So you're going to kill us the way you tried to kill Fast Nick?" Joe said.

"Nick was a fool," the auctioneer snarled. "Ramika would have paid him a fortune to come to Portugal and race Against All Odds. He could have lived like a king. But he turned it down, so I had to dispose of him. He knew too much."

Joe said, "You're not a very efficient killer. Nick's recovering from your attack. And he's already given the police a complete statement," he added, crossing his fingers.

"There'll be a warrant out for your arrest on charges of attempted murder," Frank said, jumping in. "And the U.S. has the right to retrieve criminals from Portugal. Adding four more corpses to your account won't help you a bit."

Laurence Philpin's eyes darted quickly from right to left. As suddenly as a striking snake, he reached out his free hand and grabbed Callie's arm, then held the machine pistol to her head. "You others, back off," he snarled, dragging Callie toward the motorcycle. "Keep away, or your friend won't be around much longer."

Chapter

16

CALLIE'S EYES STARED imploringly into Frank's as Philpin dragged her toward the motorcycle. The machine pistol's muzzle was pressed hard against her temple. One nervous twitch of Philpin's trigger finger and she would be dead.

"Don't even think of it!" Philpin called, an edge of hysteria in his voice. Frank could see that he was on the ragged edge of panic. They were dealing with a madman.

When he reached the motorcycle, Philpin forced Callie onto the back, then jumped on the bike. He thumbed the starter button and the engine roared to life. The rear wheel flung up a stream of mud as he fishtailed across the clearing and down a narrow track leading off from the opposite side. He didn't seem to notice when Callie pushed off the back of the motorcycle, landing in the bushes by the trail.

Frank dashed over and helped Callie to her feet. "Are you hurt?" he demanded.

"I'm okay," she gasped. "Don't let him get away."

"Not a chance," Joe yelled over his shoulder. He sprinted to the tree where Against All Odds was tethered. Yanking the reins loose, he grabbed the mane and pulled himself onto the horse's back. "Move," he shouted, digging his heels into the horse's flanks.

The horse shot up the road like a cannonball. Joe gripped with his thighs and swore that he would never complain about a bouncy ride after this. Rain pelted his face as he squinted to see the motorcycle vanishing around a long bend. What if he and Odds cut the corner? He gave a light tug on the right rein. Without missing a step, the champion steeplechaser swerved and tore into the woods.

Frank and the girls ran down the trail. As they neared the forestry gate, Frank dug into his pocket for his car keys. "Take these," he told Callie. "Call Nine-one-one on the car phone. Get the police here fast."

"What are you going to do?"

Frank closed the free end of the gate, barring

the road with the heavy steel pipe. "If Philpin decides to come back this way," he said, "he'll be in for a big surprise."

As Callie and Vanessa ran toward the van, Frank stood indecisively in the middle of the trail. How could he best help Joe corner Philpin? Too bad there wasn't another horse around.

Suddenly Frank's eyes gleamed. He ran back to the clearing and jumped into the seat of the bulldozer. It took several tries to figure out the levers that controlled the treads on each side, but soon he was lurching down the trail after Philpin and Joe. "All right!" he shouted over the whine of the diesel engine.

Joe heard the new sound from somewhere behind him, but he didn't recognize it. He was too busy dodging the tree limbs that threatened to brush him off his mount at any moment. The rain in his eyes blinded him. All he could do was point Odds in the right direction, give the horse its head, and hope to stay on. The champion seemed to run even more gracefully through the woods than he did on a track. He was a steeplechaser. Racing was in his blood.

Joe raised his head and peered through the screen of trees. "There!" he shouted. Philpin was struggling to get his heavy bike up a steep, muddy slope. Against All Odds was running parallel to the trail, about twenty yards deep in the woods. He pulled ahead of Philpin, but still Joe pushed the horse even harder. As soon as he had a large enough lead, Joe pulled Odds onto the trail and galloped straight toward Laurence Philpin.

Joe's plan was to surprise the crooked auctioneer and knock him off the bike, but Philpin saw the horse come out of the woods ahead of him.

"I'll get you, you punk!" Philpin yelled. He squeezed off a few rounds, then spun the cycle around and headed back down the hill with Joe in hot pursuit.

Frank came around a bend to see the single motorcycle headlight coming down the trail toward him. Suddenly he saw the orange flame of a muzzle flash and heard the rattle of an automatic weapon.

Desperately, Frank bent low in the seat and jammed the fourth control lever forward. The steel bulldozer's blade moved upward, shielding Frank from the whizzing bullets.

The bulldozer and the motorcycle were on a collision course. Driving blind, Frank held the center of the trail, knowing there wasn't enough room on either side for the motorcycle to pass. Philpin was trapped!

Frank heard the scream of a motorcycle engine pushed to its limits and beyond. Suddenly, like something from a circus act, the bike appeared in midair. Frank's jaw dropped as Philpin sailed right over the bulldozer. Apparently he had steered the bike at full speed up the embankment at the side of the track, then jerked back on the handlebars to become airborne.

"He's crazy," Joe said to himself, as the motorcycle took to the air. Then he realized that he was headed straight for the shovel blade. If he didn't do something fast, he was going to end up as a hood ornament for a bulldozer. He tugged on the left rein and pulled the horse into the woods once again.

"Come on, baby. Move it." Joe pressed his face next to the horse's neck as they hit top speed. He could feel the blood pulse through the awesome animal's muscles. Adrenaline was pumping through Joe's own veins so hard that he felt invincible.

Through the trees Joe could see the lights of the house. They couldn't be far from the cars. He crested a hill and watched Laurence Philpin drive at top speed directly toward the closed forestry gate. It was nothing but a steel pipe that spanned the road at hip level. "Don't do it!" Joe muttered. "If you do, there won't be anything left to put the handcuffs on."

Philpin didn't hit the barrier, though. At the last moment he swerved and laid the bike on its side, slid under the bar, then righted himself the moment he was clear.

"Who *is* this guy?" Joe wondered. Then he was approaching the barrier himself. He concentrated on sitting still and doing nothing to disturb his mount. Against All Odds flew over the gate as if he had suddenly sprouted wings. Moments later they caught up to the motorcycle. Philpin peered back over his shoulder, then aimed the machine pistol at Joe.

Joe jumped.

He leapt from the horse and crashed into Philpin's chest in a flying tackle, knocking him from the bike. They landed in thick mud. Somehow, Philpin had kept hold of the machine pistol. As he struggled to his feet he turned it on Joe and pulled the trigger.

Click.

The mud had apparently jammed the sensitive weapon. As Philpin glanced down to clear it, Joe kicked at the gun, but his foot slipped, and he went down, hard. A moment later Philpin was standing over him, preparing to stamp on Joe's neck. Joe rolled to his left and heard the foot smack the mud beside him. He grabbed Philpin's pant leg near the cuff, then smashed his fist into the side of the man's knee.

Philpin let out a nasty grunt and stepped back.

Joe climbed to his feet and squared off. What was taking Frank so long? Philpin came in with two right jabs. Joe shielded his face and absorbed the full force of the blows with his upper arms, then countered with a right cross. Philpin staggered back, then moved in to grab Joe in a bear hug, squeezing the air out of his lungs. Joe tried to force his arms outward to break the grip, but his opponent was a crazed man and his grip was steel.

Suddenly Joe arched his back and slammed his forehead against the bridge of Philpin's nose. As his opponent let go, Joe cocked his left hand and unleashed a haymaker that sent Laurence Philpin sprawling.

"Ouch," Joe said, shaking the fingers of his left hand. He could already feel the knuckles starting to swell.

Frank drove up on the bulldozer. He climbed down and hurried over. "Are you all right?" he demanded.

Joe heard sirens in the distance, growing louder. He looked down. He was covered in mud, and blood trickled from his nose. "I've been better," he said. "But you ought to see the other guy."

The next afternoon the Hardys' black van pulled into Colonel Burroughs's driveway and stopped. Vanessa jumped out, then held the door for Joe, whose left arm was in a sling. Frank and Callie followed them up the walk.

As they reached the porch, the door swung

open. Helen stood there with her Bengal tiger, Gandhi, peering around her legs.

"Hello," she said, beaming. She called over her shoulder. "Honeybear, they're here."

Frank caught Joe's gaze and raised his eyebrows in disbelief. "Honeybear?" he mouthed.

Colonel Burroughs came marching to the door with Samantha trailing behind him. While Sam hid behind her father's legs, he looked at Joe's sling and barked, "You let those doctors string you up, eh? What for?"

"I popped three knuckles," Joe replied.

"A boxer's fracture," the colonel replied. "In my day men didn't go on sick leave for that. Instead, I gave them extra KP for their bad form. Didn't anyone teach you how to punch straight?"

"Oh, be nice to him," Helen said, taking Burroughs's arm. "Admit that they did us a big favor."

"A favor?" he cried. "Nonsense! Went off on their own and paid no attention to the chain of command, that's what they did. What if everyone did that? Anarchy!"

Frank stared at him in shock. How could he be so gruff after they had just rescued his prize horse?

Suddenly Colonel Burroughs let out an enormous laugh. "You believe my guff, don't you?" he demanded with what looked a lot like a smile. "Took me seriously? No, no, boys. I know very well what a debt I owe you. And I'm not just talking about finding my horse. You returned something much more valuable to me. You convinced Helen and me to start talking again, and we were able to clear up all my petty jealousy and misunderstandings. You saved our relationship, and we're going to be married next week."

"We were hoping you could come to the ceremony," Helen said.

"We'd be honored," Joe said.

Without warning, Samantha slipped out from behind her father and leapt up into Frank's arms. Startled, he caught the child. She gave him a peck on the cheek, then wriggled free and ran back to her father's side.

"Maybe you young people can help me with another problem," Burroughs said. "Come with me." Curious, they followed him off the porch and over to the riding ring. Against All Odds was gray again, and the white marking stood out clearly on his nose. He was tacked up and feeding from the trough. As soon as he saw his owner, he headed toward the fence.

"I'm glad to see his original color," Callie said.

"Samantha and I scrubbed him all morning," Helen answered.

Burroughs put his foot on the lowest rung of the fence and said, "I've got to take my hat off to you. You solved the case when the proper authorities were getting nowhere. Chief Collig got a complete confession from that scoundrel Philpin. As for Nick, his doctors say he'll recover, but he won't be in shape to ride for a while. These modern doctors always want to keep people off their feet as long as they can."

"Brian, you're impossible!" Helen exclaimed.

"That's as may be. But meanwhile, my horse needs exercising." He picked up a riding helmet and offered it to Vanessa. "I understand you ride pretty well, young lady."

"Er—well, I manage," Vanessa stammered.

"Would you mind giving Odds his afternoon workout?" the colonel asked. "If you two get along, maybe you could make it a regular thing."

Vanessa looked at him with huge eyes. "I've always dreamed of riding this horse," she breathed. "But I never thought—"

"Doing is better than dreaming," Burroughs said, taking Helen's hand in his. "Up you go. Take him around the property, but watch for the creek in the south pasture. The water's high."

Vanessa mounted the champion stallion. She stroked his neck and bent down to whisper in his ear. Then she snapped the reins and called, "G'yup."

Against All Odds cantered once around the riding ring. As he approached the closed gate, he seemed to gather himself, then put all the power in his bunched muscles into a graceful jump. As she and her mount soared over the gate, Vanessa let out an exhilarated shout. Then they sped past the ruined barn and vanished into a green meadow.

"I never thought I'd feel jealous of a horse," Joe said, turning to Frank and Callie. "But you have to admit, that's one fine animal. I guess that proves it."

"Proves what, Joe?" Callie asked.

"Vanessa only goes for champions," Joe said.

He dodged as Frank threw a punch at his chin.

Frank and Joe's next case:

Callie's uncle Adam makes maple syrup in New Hampshire, and Callie has invited Frank and Joe to join her there for Spring Break. The idea is to go cross-country skiing—a plan that quickly goes sour. Someone has deliberately tainted the crop, and if the Hardys don't catch the culprit, Uncle Adam will soon be tapped out. But the threat to Uncle Adam's business is only the beginning. A gang has targeted other farmers in the area, and they've added two new names to their list: Frank and Joe Hardy. The boys are in the thick of it, facing bomb-throwing saboteurs and chainsaw-wielding thugs in an all-out battle to save reputations ... and save lives ... in *Pure Evil*, Case #97 in The Hardy Boys Casefiles™.

THE HARDY BOYS CASEFILES™

☐ #1: DEAD ON TARGET	73992-1/$3.99		☐ #63: COLD SWEAT	73099-1/$3.75
☐ #2: EVIL, INC.	73668-X/$3.75		☐ #64: ENDANGERED SPECIES	73100-9/$3.99
☐ #3: CULT OF CRIME	68726-3/$3.75		☐ #65: NO MERCY	73101-7/$3.99
☐ #4: THE LAZARUS PLOT	73995-6/$3.75		☐ #66: THE PHOENIX EQUATION	73102-5/$3.99
☐ #5: EDGE OF DESTRUCTION	73669-8/$3.99		☐ #67: LETHAL CARGO	73103-3/$3.75
☐ #6: THE CROWNING OF TERROR	73670-1/$3.50		☐ #68: ROUGH RIDING	73104-1/$3.75
			☐ #69: MAYHEM IN MOTION	73105-X/$3.75
☐ #7: DEATHGAME	73672-8/$3.99		☐ #70: RIGGED FOR REVENGE	73106-8/$3.75
☐ #8: SEE NO EVIL	73673-6/$3.50		☐ #71: REAL HORROR	73107-6/$3.99
☐ #9: THE GENIUS THIEVES	73674-4/$3.50		☐ #72: SCREAMERS	73108-4/$3.75
☐ #12: PERFECT GETAWAY	73675-2/$3.50		☐ #73: BAD RAP	73109-2/$3.99
☐ #13: THE BORGIA DAGGER	73676-0/$3.50		☐ #74: ROAD PIRATES	73110-6/$3.99
☐ #14: TOO MANY TRAITORS	73677-9/$3.50		☐ #75: NO WAY OUT	73111-4/$3.99
☐ #29: THICK AS THIEVES	74663-4/$3.50		☐ #76: TAGGED FOR TERROR	73112-2/$3.99
☐ #30: THE DEADLIEST DARE	74613-8/$3.50		☐ #77: SURVIVAL RUN	79461-2/$3.99
☐ #32: BLOOD MONEY	74665-0/$3.50		☐ #78: THE PACIFIC CONSPIRACY	79462-0/$3.99
☐ #33: COLLISION COURSE	74666-9/$3.50		☐ #79: DANGER UNLIMITED	79463-9/$3.99
☐ #35: THE DEAD SEASON	74105-5/$3.50		☐ #80: DEAD OF NIGHT	79464-7/$3.99
☐ #37: DANGER ZONE	73751-1/$3.75		☐ #81: SHEER TERROR	79465-5/$3.99
☐ #41: HIGHWAY ROBBERY	70038-3/$3.75		☐ #82: POISONED PARADISE	79466-3/$3.99
☐ #42: THE LAST LAUGH	74614-6/$3.50		☐ #83: TOXIC REVENGE	79467-1/$3.99
☐ #44: CASTLE FEAR	74615-4/$3.75		☐ #84: FALSE ALARM	79468-X/$3.99
☐ #45: IN SELF-DEFENSE	70042-1/$3.75		☐ #85: WINNER TAKE ALL	79469-8/$3.99
☐ #46: FOUL PLAY	70043-X/$3.75		☐ #86: VIRTUAL VILLAINY	79470-1/$3.99
☐ #47: FLIGHT INTO DANGER	70044-8/$3.75		☐ #87: DEAD MAN IN DEADWOOD	79471-X/$3.99
☐ #48: ROCK 'N' REVENGE	70045-6/$3.50		☐ #88: INFERNO OF FEAR	79472-8/$3.99
☐ #49: DIRTY DEEDS	70046-4/$3.99		☐ #89: DARKNESS FALLS	79473-6/$3.99
☐ #50: POWER PLAY	70047-2/$3.99		☐ #90: DEADLY ENGAGEMENT	79474-4/$3.99
☐ #52: UNCIVIL WAR	70049-9/$3.50		☐ #91: HOT WHEELS	79475-2/$3.99
☐ #53: WEB OF HORROR	73089-4/$3.99		☐ #92: SABOTAGE AT SEA	79476-0/$3.99
☐ #54: DEEP TROUBLE	73090-8/$3.99		☐ #93: MISSION: MAYHEM	88204-X/$3.99
☐ #55: BEYOND THE LAW	73091-6/$3.50		☐ #94: A TASTE FOR TERROR	88205-8/$3.99
☐ #56: HEIGHT OF DANGER	73092-4/$3.99		☐ #95: ILLEGAL PROCEDURE	88206-6/$3.99
☐ #57: TERROR ON TRACK	73093-2/$3.99		☐ #96: AGAINST ALL ODDS	88207-4/$3.99
☐ #60: DEADFALL	73096-7/$3.75			
☐ #61: GRAVE DANGER	73097-5/$3.99			
☐ #62: FINAL GAMBIT	73098-3/$3.75			